2 NOVELLAS FROM THE TAYLOR JACKSON SERIES

J.T. ELLISON

TWO TALES PRESS

NEW YORK TIMES BESTSELLING AUTHOR

J.T. ELLISON

"Shocking suspense, compelling characters and fascinating forensic details."

—#1 *New York Times* bestselling author Lisa Gardner on *A Deeper Darkness*

BLOOD SUGAR BABY

A TAYLOR JACKSON NOVELLA

1

Nashville, Tennessee

He was lost. His GPS didn't take roadwork into account, nor roads closed to accommodate protests; he'd been shunted off onto several side streets and was driving in circles. He finally made a right turn and pulled to the curb to get out a real map, and as he reached into the glove box— shit, he needed to get that knife out of there—he saw her. She was on the concrete sidewalk, sprawled back against the wall, a spread of multicolored blankets at her feet, staring vacantly into space. Her dirty blond hair was past limp and fell into dreadlocks, matted against her skull on the left side. He drove past slowly, watching, seeing the curve of her skull beneath the clumps of hair; the slope of her jaw; her neat little ear, surprisingly white and clean, nestled against her grimy skin. Her eyes were light. He was too far away to see if they were blue or green. Light irises, and unfocused pupils. High, perhaps, or starved, or simply beyond caring.

Perfect.

No one would miss her. And he could rid himself of this nagging fury that made him so damn antsy.

He closed the glove box and circled the block. There she sat, just waiting for him.

A sign.

A gift.

It had been a bad day. The fat ass he'd started med school with, Heath Stover, had called, wanting to get together. Stover was a classic jock gone to seed: flakily jovial, always over-the-top, clearly trying to compensate for something. JR had run into him last month in New Orleans, been forced into drinking hurricanes at Pat O'Briens, and had stupidly told Stover where he worked.

He shook his head, the scene replaying itself over and over and over. Stover bragging and braying at the top of his lungs about his hugely successful practice, his new BMW, his long-legged, big-busted bride, his offer of tenure at Tulane. The only thing off in his brilliant, wonderful life, Stover confided, was his piece on the side, who'd been pushing him to leave his wife.

In the moment, bolstered by alcohol, the camaraderie, the overwhelming need to fit in, to be accepted, to look as palatable to the real world as this fuck-up, he cast sanity aside. Arrogance overtook him, and he revealed his own career path, one that had taken him up the ladder at Bosco Blades; he was a salesman extraordinaire. No Willy Loman, though he perhaps looked and sounded a bit like the sad sack, but that was all a part of his act. He was better than that. Better than good. He was the best the company had: stock options, access to the corporate jet, the house in Aspen, all of it.

"As a matter of fact," he'd told Stover, "I'm headlining a conference in Nashville next month. Talking about the new laser-guided scalpel we've developed. Hell of a thing."

"Hell of a thing," Stover had replied. He was counting on

the fact that Stover was far too drunk to recall the name of the company, and he gave him a fake number to write down, and a bogus email.

But the stupid son of a bitch had remembered the company name, had called and wormed JR's personal cell number out of his secretary, and managed to put himself on JR's calendar. In a couple of hours, the sloth would be waiting at a restaurant several streets away for an instant replay of their recent night in the Big Easy.

If only Stover knew what had really happened that night. About the knife, the silent scream, the ease with which the flesh accepted his blade.

He needed someplace quiet and calm to prepare himself for his night out with a "friend." He needed a drink, truth be told. Many drinks.

But the woman would do just as well. She would turn his frown upside down.

He parked a few blocks away, pulled a baseball cap low on his head, and walked back to the spot. A marble and concrete sign said he was at Legislative Plaza. The War Memorial. The Capitol rose to his right, high against the blue sky, and the small crowd of protestors with their signs held high gathered on the stairs. He needed to be careful when he passed them, not to draw their attention.

He found the perfect spot halfway down the block, shielded from the friendly mob on the stairs, and from the street, with the trident maples as cover.

And then he watched. And waited. At some point, she would have to move, and then he would follow, and strike.

To hell with Heath Stover. He had a rendezvous ahead with someone much more enticing.

2

The homicide offices in Nashville's Criminal Justice Center had been quiet all day. It was the first Monday off daylight savings time, and even though it was barely 5:00 p.m., the skies outside Lieutenant Taylor Jackson's window were an inky black. The lights over the Jefferson Street Bridge glowed, warm and homey, and she could just see the slice of river flowing north to Kentucky. It was a moonless night; the vapor lamps' illuminations reflected against the black waters.

Her detectives were gone for the day. Paperwork had been completed; cases were being worked to her satisfaction. She'd stuck around regardless—the B-shift detectives would be here shortly, and she could hand off the department to her new sergeant, Bob Parks. He was a good match for the position and had the respect of her team, who'd worked with him for years. Parks had no illusions about moving up the ladder; he was content to be her sergeant until his twenty was up in two years and he retired. His son, Brent, was on the force now, too. Taylor suspected Parks had opted to get off the streets to give his son some room. Classy guy.

Her desk phone rang, cutting through the quiet, and she shifted in the window, suddenly filled with premonition.

"Lieutenant Jackson."

It was Marcus Wade, one of her detectives.

"Hey, Loot. We've got a problem."

"What kind of problem?"

"The kind that comes with the chief of police attached."

"I thought you went home."

"I was heading that way, but saw a cordon by Legislative Plaza where the protestors have been camped. Looked like something we might be called in on. I was right."

Taylor took a seat, opened her notebook. "What's going on?"

"They found one of the Occupy Nashville folks dead, right at the steps to the War Memorial Auditorium. Stab wound to the chest. Nice and neat, too."

Taylor groaned.

"It gets better."

"What?"

"The victim? It's Go-Go Dunham."

"Oh, son of a bitch."

"Yep. You wanna head on down here?"

"I'll be there in ten. Who all's there?"

"A shit load of protestors right now. Someone got in touch with her dad, so he's on his way. I called you first. I know you're gonna want to tell the chief."

"Oh, Marcus, you're just too kind."

"You know it," he said, and clicked off.

Normally Taylor's captain, Joan Huston, would be handling the chief, but she was out on paid leave—her first grandchild had just been born, and she'd taken some time to go be with her daughter.

Taylor hung up the phone and grabbed her leather jacket from the peg behind her door. She shrugged into the well-worn coat, retied her hair in a ponytail, grabbed her radio and set off. She took the stairs to the chief's office two at a time.

Virginia "Go-Go" Dunham was the twenty-two-year-old daughter of Joe Dunham, founder of one of the biggest healthcare companies in Nashville. His latest headline-grabbing venture was building environmentally-friendly dialysis centers, ones designed to be both pleasing to the patients and capture major tax breaks from the government. The trend had caught on— his designs had been patented and utilized to build similar centers across the country. Dunham was a pillar of the community, a regular at all the major charitable events, a contributor to the mayor's election fund, and an all-around connected guy. His one and only daughter, Virginia, known as Go-Go, had felt living up to her dad's squeaky-clean image too much trouble, and, as a difficult youngster, quickly mired herself in the social drug scene. She'd earned her moniker at fourteen, when she'd been busted dancing at the Déjà Vu strip club. This was before the new ordinance forbade touching the dancers, and nubile, blond, busty Go-Go had taken full advantage of the situation. She was pulling down three grand a night, and putting the vast majority of that cash right back up her nose.

Several stints in rehab and a few busts later, she was supposed to have cleaned up her act. No longer a regular fixture on the nightclub scene, she'd gone back to school, earned a degree and taken a job working for her dad.

If she were still straight, how in the world had she managed to get herself dead?

Lights were on in the chief's office. This wasn't going to go over well. He was a close personal friend of the victim's father. As close and personal as anyone could be when they were involved in political endeavors together. Dunham and the mayor were fishing buddies; she knew the chief tagged along on occasion.

The offices were empty and quiet, the admin gone home for the day. Taylor was about to knock on the chief's closed door when he called out, "I hear you lurking out there, Lieutenant. Come in."

She followed his instruction.

Chief DeMike was a veteran of the force, promoted to the head spot from within, and a welcome change from the previous incarnation, a man as corrupt as the day was long. DeMike's hair was white, his face ruddy, with cheeks and jowls that would swing in a stiff breeze. He looked a bit like an overweight Bassett hound masquerading as Santa Claus in dress blues. But he was good police, and had always been fair with her.

"You're here about the Dunham girl?"

"You already know?"

DeMike pulled a cigar out of his humidor and started playing with it. "Sugar, I know everything in this town."

Taylor raised an eyebrow.

"Sorry." He snipped off the end of the cigar, then rammed it into the corner of his mouth. He couldn't smoke it in here, not that he hadn't before, but Taylor knew it was only a comfort gesture.

"Joe's been notified. We need to head down to the scene. He's going to meet us there. He's expecting a full show, so you should be prepared."

"I am. Not a problem. But tell me, who made the call to Mr. Dunham? Seems a bit quick to me."

"Already investigating, Lieutenant? Good. I like that. He told me one of her friends called him. Apparently, she's been camping out down there with the protestors."

He stood, the bulk of his weight tossing his chair backward against the windowsill with a crash.

"I thought she'd been walking the straight and narrow of late."

"I don't know, Lieutenant. Head on down there and find out. I'll arrive with due pomp and circumstance in a few."

Taylor nodded gravely, trying not to smile. "Yes, sir."

3

When the first siren lit up the night, he was four blocks away, at Rippy's on Broadway, sipping a Yuengling, a pulled pork sandwich smothered in sweet and tangy BBQ sauce and corn cakes with butter on order, waiting for Stover to show. The high-pitched wail made pride blossom in his chest.

It had gone gloriously. She'd never seen him coming. As he predicted, after an hour, she'd shuffled off toward the port-a-potties, and when she'd drawn near, he'd straightened his spine, let the knife slide into his hand, and stepped from the bushes. He'd become so adept at his trade that the contact he'd had with her was, on the surface, just an incidental bump. As he'd said, "Excuse me," he'd slid the knife right up under her breastbone directly into her heart. A clean cut, in and out, no twisting or sawing. Precision. Perfection.

He was half a block down the street before she hit the sidewalk.

He was so good at this. Granted, practice does make perfect, and he'd had quite a bit of practice.

He allowed himself a smile. He'd managed to salvage a

very annoying day, and give himself something wonderful to think about tonight. Something to chase away the annoyance of having to play charades with Stover the fat ass tonight.

Stupid bastard. Who was more successful in their *chosen* fields?

Now, JR, stop worrying about that. Think about what you just did, how you're sitting right under their noses, having a nice little Southern dinner. Think about the edge of the blade, colored a grimy rust by the girl's blood, sitting in your pocket. Think about the way the tip fed into her flesh, and her eyes caught yours, and she knew it was you who was ending her life. These are appropriate thoughts. You can't look back to the bad things. Just stay focused on the here and now.

Stover arrived with a bellow.

JR played his part—accepting the rough handshake, making small talk, eating, drinking, pretending—all the while sustaining himself with thoughts of his light-eyed beauty, lying on the sidewalk, her heart giving one last gush of blood to her body.

After what seemed like hours, Stover called for the bill, belched loudly without covering his mouth and announced, "We need women."

The idea was repugnant to JR. Women were not for defiling one's self with, they were for the glory of the knife. Glory be. Glorious. Glory glory glorious.

Perhaps he'd had one beer too many.

But this event presented his best chance of escape. So he acquiesced, and followed Stover into the night. The street outside the restaurant was hopping, busy with tourists and revelers even on a Monday. Downtown Nashville was a twenty-four/seven world, and they slipped into the throngs without causing a second glance. Because JR fit right in. He always fit in now.

4

Taylor arrived at the crime scene ten minutes after Marcus's call. The site was just down the street from the CJC; she could have walked it if she wasn't in too much of a hurry. But tonight she was. Containment would be key. The Occupy Nashville protestors had been causing an uproar downtown for two weeks now. Bills were being passed to stop their ability to gather freely, face-offs between the protestors and other groups had turned the mood on the steps sour, and even the people of Nashville who agreed with their agenda were beginning to turn against them.

The real beneficiaries of their protest were the homeless who spent their time hanging out in the little park on Capitol Boulevard, burrowed in between the downtown Library and Legislative Plaza. Strangely enough, the hippies and the homeless looked remarkably alike, and do-gooders answering the call of the protesters by traveling downtown to bring food and blankets didn't necessarily know the difference. The homeless weren't stupid; they took full advantage of the situation. They were being fed, clothed, and warmed daily, sharing smokes and tents with the protestors. Taylor didn't think that was such a bad thing, but she did wish the folks who'd rallied to the call would think to provide this kind of succor to those less fortunate on a more regular basis. If Twitter could take down a despot, surely it could help keep Nashville's homeless clothed and fed.

But that wasn't her problem right now. She needed to contain a huge local story before it got blown into a political mess.

She was an experienced detective—fourteen years on the job with Metro—so she knew better than to jump to conclusions. If Go-Go was with the protestors and had been stabbed, chances were she'd been murdered by one of her fellow demonstrators. And that news was going to go national.

As she parked, she took in the scene, one she'd been privy to too many times. Sixth Street was blockaded between Church and Charlotte, blue and white lights flashing crazily on the concrete buildings, reflecting off the black glass of the Tennessee Performing Arts Center. Thankfully TPAC didn't have anything playing tonight, the building's lobby was dark and gloomy. She could see the focus of all the attention was midway up the street, just below the steps to the Plaza.

"Lieutenant!"

Tim Davis, the head of Metro's Crime Scene unit, waved to Taylor. She waved back and headed his way, watching the crowd as she walked down Sixth. The area had been cordoned off—that's what Marcus had seen driving home— but a large crowd had gathered on either side of the crime scene. Yellow tape headed them off, but frightened eyes peered down from the Plaza, and across from TPAC a small horde of people had formed, staring curiously up the street in hopes of seeing something tawdry.

Tim was overseeing the evidence gathering. She was glad

to see him on duty. Tim was meticulous, and if there was evidence to find, he'd make sure it was bagged and tagged.

"Hey, man. What's up?"

"Marcus told you it was Go-Go?"

"Yeah. Damn shame. What's the evidence telling us?"

"Single stab wound to the chest. I've been collecting everything around, but the ground's littered with crap from the protestors. Messy bunch of people." His nose wrinkled in disapproval. Tim liked things straight and clean. It's what made him so good at spotting objects that were out of place.

"We've got cameras here, don't we?"

"Yeah. I've got a call into TPAC. Their security footage will give us the best chance of seeing what happened."

"Good. Let me know if you find anything else. Is that Keri working the body?"

"Yeah. Sure do miss Sam."

"You and me both, my friend." Sam was Dr. Samantha Owens, Taylor's best friend and the former head of Forensic Medical, the lead medical examiner for the Mid-State of Tennessee. She'd recently moved to Washington, D.C., and Taylor missed her dreadfully. She understood. God knew she understood. If she'd been faced with the kind of loss Sam experienced, she'd have run away, too. But she couldn't help missing her like hell.

"Have you heard from her?"

"I did, a couple of days ago. She's doing well. Found a place she likes in Georgetown."

"Good. Next time you talk to her, give her my best. I'm going to start running some of the evidence we collected. I'll shout if we get anything that looks relevant."

Taylor glanced at her watch—5:15 p.m. The chief would be down here soon. She needed to hurry up and get him some info he could use for a presser. The chief did so love to be on air, and if they hurried, he could make the 6:00 news.

Keri McGee was on her knees next to the body. Taylor joined her.

"Yo," Keri said.

"Yo back. What do you have for me?"

"A whole lot of nothing. No trauma to the body, outside of the stab wound, of course. I'm about finished here, actually. She's only been dead for a little while, no more than an hour. She was found quickly. Was she living on the streets?"

"Why do you ask?"

"Newspaper in her shoes and socks. They do that for warmth. And she hasn't bathed in a while. Not that that's any real indication, a bunch of these folks have been camping down here for days."

Taylor took her own inventory of Go-Go. That the girl hadn't bathed recently was quite evident. She looked like she'd been living rough: her skin was brown with dirt, she had no jewelry on, no watch, just a small red thread tied around her right wrist. From her matted hair to her grubby clothes, Go-Go was downright filthy. She didn't look much like the other protestors, who, despite their attempts to blend in, still glowed with health.

"I want to talk to whoever found her."

"Over there," Keri said, pointing at a young man who was hovering nearby. "I'm about ready to take her back to the morgue. Fox will autopsy her in the morning, along with everyone else we loaded up on today."

"Sounds good. Thanks."

Taylor took her turn with the kid who'd found the body next. He couldn't be a day over twenty, with a snippet of a beard, dark hair and dark eyes, shoulders hunched into a hooded North Face fleece. Taylor appreciated the irony. The kid was protesting capitalism wearing a two-hundred-dollar jacket. His face was streaked with tears.

"Hey there. I'm Lieutenant Jackson, homicide. What's your name?"

"Derek Rucka."

"How do you know Go-Go?"

"She's my girlfriend."

"Really? You're dating? She doesn't seem to be in very good shape for a girl with a man."

He looked down. "She *was* my girlfriend. We broke up a few weeks ago. She took off, and I hadn't seen her until today. I was down here with the gang and I saw her smoking on the steps. We chatted."

"About what?"

"Her coming home. She, well, if you know her name, you know her history. Go-Go is bipolar. She's been doing really well, too, working for her dad. That's where we met. My mom is on dialysis. But she stopped taking her meds about a month ago, and things went downhill pretty quickly."

"So you were out here trying to save her?"

He shook his head miserably. "No. Not at all. I didn't know she was out here. I certainly didn't know she was on the streets. I'd have come looking sooner."

"So today of all days, you just happen to run into her, and then boom, she's dead? Is there something you want to tell me, Derek?"

The boy's face flushed with horror, and his mouth dropped open. "What? No. I didn't do anything to her. We just talked. Shared a bowl. That's it."

"So you admit to doing drugs with the deceased?"

The kid nodded, his head moving vigorously on its slender stalk. "Yeah. But I promise, that's all we did."

"I think you should probably come down to my office and talk to me some more, Derek. Okay?"

The bowed shoulders straightened and the tears stopped. His voice grew cold. "Am I under arrest?"

"Not right now. We're just going to have a little chat."

"I know my rights. You can't detain me unless you have cause."

Taylor narrowed her eyes at the boy.

"Don't give me a reason, kid. I'm not in the mood. We can do this hard, or we can do this easy. You just admitted to using an illegal substance on state property. You want to go down on a drug charge, I'm happy to make that happen for you. Or you can come in and have a nice friendly chat. Your call."

She stepped back a foot and fingered her cuffs. Rucka swallowed and shoved his hands in his pockets, head cast downward in defeat.

"Okay then. Come with me." Taylor led the kid to her car, put him in the back seat. "I'll be back in a minute. You just hang out."

Of course, one of the reporters saw this, and shouted across the tape at Taylor frantically. "Lieutenant, do you have a suspect in custody?"

Taylor ignored her. She wasn't about to get in a conversation with a reporter, not when the chief was on his way. No sense stealing the old man's glory. She returned to the body, watched as Keri McGee took samples and bagged the girl's hands.

"Anything?" Taylor asked.

"Not really. Nothing that's leaping out. I have hairs that don't match the body, debris, but that's not a surprise, considering she's out in the crowd like this. She's wrapped up like she's wearing a sari. I'll get her back to the morgue, and we can get her peeled down to her skin, run everything and see what's out of place."

One of these things is not like the other . . .

Oh, great. Now she was going to be singing that stupid song for the rest of the night.

Taylor didn't blame Keri for wanting to get the girl out of the limelight as quickly as possible, especially with the chief on the way. It was practically record speed for a homicide investigation, but Keri was a stellar death investigator. Taylor trusted her to know when it was time to move on to the next step.

Go-Go would be posted in the morning, along with any other unfortunates who found their way to the tables of Forensic Medical. In the meantime, Taylor had a job to do. She'd started toward the perimeter when Keri shouted to her.

Taylor turned and saw Keri waving her back.

"What's up?"

Keri handed Taylor a small leather wallet. "Found it under her layers of blanket. Don't know why I didn't see it when I rolled her."

"Hers?"

"Not unless her name is James Gustafson."

Taylor flipped the wallet open. It was all the standard stuff: a driver's license and a few credit cards, plus some cash. The photo showed a pale man, forty-one, blue on brown, five foot ten inches. His address showed him to be from Virginia.

"Keri, tell me if I'm crazy. Maybe we just caught a break, and this is our killer's wallet. Go-Go tried picking his pocket, he got pissed and stabbed her, then was spooked and ran before he retrieved it?"

"Would you leave your wallet if you had just stabbed someone?"

"No one said these guys were geniuses."

Keri laughed, then a frown crossed her face. She had her purple-nitrile-gloved hands in the grubby folds of Go-Go's blankets. "Ick. Now that's weird."

"What?" Taylor asked.

Keri produced three more wallets, all very similar to the first, and four cell phones.

"Well, well, well," Taylor said. "Our Go-Go is quite the little pickpocket."

"Bet there's some folks up on the plaza who will be happy to get their stuff back."

"No kidding. Good job, Keri. I'll have Parks Jr. do some canvassing, see which phone and wallet belongs to which person. They can all come in and have a chat. At least we have some suspects. Maybe we can crack this one tonight. Later, 'gator."

Taylor headed back to the perimeter tape, planning out the evening, and trying to formulate exactly what she was going to say to Go-Go's father about his wayward, now dead daughter.

What a damn shame.

5

"Whoo-eeeee!"

Stover had decided to ride the mechanical bull at the Cadillac Ranch. He was spinning in circles, whooping and hollering and generally making an ass of himself. Two bleached blond bimbos had attached themselves to him about an hour earlier, and they gazed adoringly at their man for the evening, salivating over his generosity and the size of his wallet.

JR couldn't stand this much longer. He glanced at his watch; it was past midnight. When had that happened? Granted, he'd been drinking. Keeping up with Stover was a challenge for a man who generally didn't allow himself to indulge in more than the occasional adult beverage, and only then as a reward. Funny, he'd broken his own rules twice in a month. What did that say? Was he getting lax? Tired? Old?

No. Never old. Not in that way. He was certainly aging, like any normal person would, but he was far from staid and predictable.

Stover, now he was predictable. Out of town, away from his wife—and his mistress—looking to grab the first piece of tail that would bite, throw back as much drink as his protruding gut would allow, then fuck and pass out in a strange room without a second thought.

JR was better than that. Cleaner. Seemlier. And certainly more temperate. Stover drew attention to himself like a five-year-old throwing a tantrum—everyone around was aware of him. JR never could handle that level of attention from strangers. Not that he wanted to. God, if he were this indiscreet, he'd have landed in a jail cell years ago. No, prudence and moderation were the keys to his longevity.

Almost as if Stover could read his mind, the man started yelling in a drunken slur. "JR." The name came out *Jar*. "Ca'mere. Get yer bony ass up here."

The blondes twittered and simpered.

JR waved him off, then realized how incredibly intoxicated Stover was. After his invitation, he'd closed his eyes and started to slide off the back of the bull.

It was time to go.

He turned and walked to the bar to settle the bill. Stover had given the bartender his credit card to hold to keep the tab open. JR asked for the tab, and told the bartender to keep it on the card. He figured Stover might as well pay for the drinks, considering how inconsiderate he was being.

But the bartender came back and told JR the card had been declined. Cursing silently, he reached for his own wallet. He'd just give the man some cash, and be done with it.

His back right pocket was empty.

Son of a bitch.

He glanced over to the women who'd latched on to them, but couldn't see either of them in the crowd.

Fury began to build in his chest, so hard and fast that the bartender reared back when he saw the look on JR's face. He'd been ripped off. The worthless bitches had stolen his wallet and run.

He went to Stover, who'd just tripped off the bull, and grabbed him by the shirtfront.

JR hissed the words. "They stole my wallet, you fat fuck."

"Sucks for you." Stover began to laugh, the hysterical giggles of a drunken hyena, which just pissed JR off more. He dragged the man to the bar, pushed him roughly against the wooden rail.

"Your card was declined. Pay the tab."

Something in JR's voice registered with Stover. He obeyed immediately, pulled his wallet out—he still had his, the shit —and paid for their drinks with two crisp $100 bills.

Satisfied, JR stalked away. He needed to find those women. The last thing he wanted was his name getting out. Granted, it wasn't his real name on the license and credit cards, but a variation, a pseudonym, if you will, something he used to assure his anonymity as he cruised the country. He'd adopted the name when he failed out of med school. Employers wouldn't be inclined to hire a man who they perceived wasn't even competent enough to finish school. That wasn't it, wasn't it at all. He could have done the work if he wanted to, but he'd found another hobby, one that satisfied him in ways being a doctor never would. He made a show of struggling with the work so his classmates would think he was just incapable, and he could fade away from their lives.

But Stover was his Achilles heel. He knew JR's real name. The idiot had spied him in the hotel in New Orleans and remembered.

JR pulled up short at the door to the street. The women became secondary. That was a problem, but it wasn't fatal. He knew what he needed to do. There was only one way to really fix this mess.

Stover had to die.

He felt a tingle of excitement go through his body.

Two in one day? In one city? Dare he?

His mind answered in the affirmative, with a caveat.

Don't use the knife.

JR waited for Stover to catch up to him, his mind racing. So many ways to die. Fall in front of a car, trip and hit your head on a light pole . . .

He thought about his drive around the city earlier and it hit him. The river was only a block away. There were three bridges, too, one of which was solely for pedestrians.

JR assessed the man beside him. He was drunk enough. He'd never be able to swim.

It wouldn't have the satisfaction of the knife—nothing could top that—but this would solve one very large, loud, nagging problem.

He turned to his old friend.

"Come on, Heath. Let's go for a walk."

Stover fell into step beside him, yammering away. God, did the man ever shut his trap?

Well, JR, give him this. It is his last will and testament, after all.

It only took five minutes to mount the bridge and cross halfway to the highest point. He stopped to admire the view. They were standing over the murky river water, the lights of Nashville shining majestically in the darkness.

Time to say goodbye.

He didn't mean to do it. He really didn't. JR gave Stover a push, and the drunken fool began to struggle, and there was nothing to be done for it. The blade was in his hand before he even gave it a second thought. JR shoved the knife in quickly, then drew it out. The pain was enough to stop Stover's cries. He didn't move for a moment, looking vaguely surprised, then toppled over the edge of the bridge himself, with no effort whatsoever.

JR did something he'd only done once before, in another

moment of extreme distress. He tossed the knife off the bridge after Stover's body. It killed him to do it—my God, what a prize for his collection, a blade that took not one, but two lives, in a single day—but he'd been forced into impulsivity here in Nashville, and like any animal who knew it had just survived a close call, he needed to retreat to his bolt hole and lick his wounds.

He would call the conference organizers first thing in the morning and plead a bad case of food poisoning. In the meantime, he needed to cut his losses and get the hell out of Dodge.

Nashville had been a little too good to him.

6

Taylor spent Monday evening keeping the wheels in motion on Go-Go's murder. She had a long, sad chat with Joe Dunham, promised him she'd do everything in her power to bring Go-Go's killer to justice as quickly as possible. It wasn't an empty promise; she had several solid leads already. She was confident she'd have her man soon.

Derek Rucka's interrogation gave her absolutely squat, outside of the fact that Go-Go had been known to suffer from a wee bit of kleptomania, and going off her meds had exacerbated the syndrome. She was a pack rat, indiscriminately lifting whatever she could get her hands on: wallets and phones mostly, but brushes, lipsticks, pens—anything that could be separated from its owner. According to Rucka, it was purely for fun; she took a perverse pleasure in getting away with it.

The kid's story checked out, and a canvas of the protestors confirmed that he was on the other side of the memorial when Go-Go went down. Taylor cut him loose just after midnight.

They'd also found all the wallet and cell phone owners,

save one: Gustafson. Everyone else checked out. Taylor had that niggling feeling in the back of her head that there was something to this guy. It was something in his eyes. Alone at her desk, she stared at his license photo for a few minutes, then ran him through the system. Clean. She found a phone number and called, but the phone just rang and rang and rang.

Instinct is vital for every homicide detective, and hers was on fire. She called the local precinct that serviced the area where Gustafson lived in Virginia, but it was late, and they were busy working their own cases. Someone would get back to her tomorrow, supposedly. She knew well enough that she'd have to call back in the morning, made a note of it on her list.

She'd lock him down tomorrow. Frustrated, she headed home.

John Baldwin, her fiancé, an FBI profiler, was in Minnesota working a case, so Taylor had the house to herself. Sleep never came easy for her, with or without Baldwin's presence, but she'd grown accustomed to having him in her bed while she gazed at the ceiling, at the very least to warm her chilly feet. With both he and Sam gone, she was a bit lonely. But instead of wallowing, she grabbed a beer from the fridge, racked up a game of nine-ball and expertly shot the balls down one by one, until she finally began to weary around three. She slept a couple of fitful hours, then got up, showered and headed to Forensic Medical for Go-Go's autopsy.

Taylor attended herself so the chief could have instant updates to share with his high-profile friends. It was an unremarkable event and only served to make her miss Sam more. Dr. Fox was a good ME, quick and to the point, but he lacked that little bit extra, the sixth sense Sam seemed to have for making a murder come to life. The girl had been stabbed once, the knife most likely a seven-to-eight-inch, double-bladed stiletto, sliding right past her ribs, under her breast-bone, and into her heart. THC showed on the tox screen; a more complete report would take weeks. Exsanguination was the official cause of death, and it was ruled a homicide.

Taylor felt sorry for Go-Go. She was obviously a very troubled girl, but not one who deserved to die on the street at the wrong end of a blade.

It was still early when Fox finished the post. Taylor debated stopping at Waffle House and getting breakfast, but decided to go back to the office first, which ended up being a good call. The videos from TPAC were waiting on her, with a note from Tim: "Check out 3:47 p.m. Think we may have a shot of our guy. I'm in court, will be over as soon as I'm done."

Taylor popped the disc into her laptop and hit Play.

The footage was surprisingly clear, though in muted black and white. She dragged the bar to the spot Tim suggested and hit play. It took three replays to see it. Damn, Tim had a good eye. There was a flash of white in the bottom right edge of the screen, which Taylor figured must be the bill of a hat. Her theory was confirmed a moment later when a man walked through the full frame, wearing a white baseball cap. He stepped right into a bundle of rags that Taylor assumed must have been Go-Go, then disappeared out of the frames. Go-Go dropped to the ground, and that was it. A fraction of a second. And the bastard's back to the camera the whole time.

Well, the tapes had at least narrowed her search down to the male species. That cut out fifty percent of the suspect pool.

She did some quick mental measuring, putting the guy against the stone wall that led to the auditorium and figured he wasn't over six feet. That Gustafson fellow was about that height as well.

She played the tape several more times, but couldn't find anything more. The idea that Go-Go had managed to pick the man's pocket as he stabbed her looked incredibly remote. It was a blitz attack, fast, clean. Professional even. And if it was his wallet, he certainly didn't attempt to retrieve it. He hit the girl, knocked her down and was gone in the blink of an eye.

Maybe Taylor was barking up the wrong tree here.

Her phone rang, interrupting her thoughts, and she glanced down to see the cell number of her new sergeant. She answered, "Jackson."

"Hey, Loot. It's Parks. I'm down here on River Road boat ramp. We have a floater. ID on him says his name is Heath Stover, late of the Big Easy."

"Bully for you. Call Wade, he's on. I'm working Go-Go."

Parks said, "I know you are. I've already got Wade here. But this is something you might want to see. Our New Orleans dude? He's been stabbed. Right in the same spot as Go-Go."

7

Heath Stover's overweight torso bore a familiar mark, just under his sternum, a slash in the flesh that allowed the yellow subcutaneous fat to squish out around the edges of the wound. The water had washed the blood away. Fox got on the autopsy immediately once the body arrived at Forensic Medical, and Taylor stood to the side, watching, arms crossed, tapping the toe of her boot on the floor while Fox measured and murmured and inserted a special ruler into the slit to determine its depth. He finally stood and nodded.

"Same kind of blade. Double edged, sharp as hell. See how there's no hesitation, or wiggle room? Went straight in, under the sternum and into the heart." Fox stood up and looked at Taylor, his brown eyes troubled. "I have to tell you, Lieutenant, whoever did this knew what he was doing."

"Is it the same person who killed Go-Go?"

"I can't tell you that. But he—or she—knew exactly where to place the blade for maximum effectiveness. This isn't your every day stabbing. It's clean, precise, and done with amazing skill. And Go-Go's was exactly the same."

"I think we're safe saying *he*. I believe we have Go-Go's murder on tape. If she hadn't gone down I'd have thought he just bumped into her. It was quick. Here, help me run this through."

They played out the scenario she'd seen on the tape a few times, and Fox confirmed that based on Go-Go's wound, the stabbing could definitely work the way Taylor had seen on the videotape.

Fox turned back to his newest guest. "But Stover here, he got stabbed, then went in the river somewhere. Wasn't in the water too long, and there is water in his lungs, just a bit. He was on his last legs when he went in, but he was alive. Could be your blitz attacker hit him and he went in the water, or he killed him by the bank and pushed him over the edge. Radiographs show he does have a few broken bones, so he either got in a fight, or fell—"

Taylor stopped tapping her foot. "Off one of the bridges. That would explain the broken bones. We can do a current analysis from last night, see where he might have gone into the river."

"That makes sense to me. Huh. If this is the same killer, he did two in one day. Dude's got a serious problem."

"No kidding. Thanks, Fox. Now I have to go put Stover and Go-Go together, find out what they have in common. Then I can figure out who did this to them both."

The words floated to her head again, this time slightly altered.

One of these things is *too much* like the other.

8

Taylor spent the drive back to the office in deep thought. Two kills, exactly alike, with two people who, on the surface, had absolutely nothing in common. A quick investigation on Stover found that he was in town on business, had checked into the Hermitage Hotel in the late afternoon, asked directions to Rippy's BBQ on Broadway, then, around six the previous evening, set off on foot toward LoBro. Marcus Wade was down there now, nosing around. Hopefully there'd be a lead.

In the meantime, Taylor set to work getting in touch with the Fairfax County Police in Virginia. A few annoying false starts later, she was finally connected to a detective named Drake Hagerman. Taylor laid out the story and asked for his help tracking down Gustafson. He promised to get back to her within the day. Satisfied, Taylor hung up and called Marcus to see what was shaking on his end.

What was shaking, apparently, was pay dirt. Marcus answered in a huff.

"I was just about to call you. Can you send me a picture of

the guy whose wallet Go-Go had, the one we didn't find last night?"

"I'll bring it down myself. Why? You got something?"

"Stover was in here last night, dining with another guy. Description sounds an awful lot like that photo on the license. If it's him ... "

Taylor felt that flash of excitement she got when a case was about to break wide open. Less than twenty-four hours. Impressive. Her people were damn good at their jobs.

"I'll be there in five."

She called Chief DeMike and let him know what was happening, then set off down to Rippy's.

The bar was packed full, the lunch crowd rolling in food and drink and overly loud country music. Taylor would love to know how much they pulled down in a year; Rippy's was always packed to the gills.

She found Marcus at the back bar, chatting with a pony-tailed, jean-clad waitress. He looked quite pleased with himself. Marcus was adorable, and his good looks sometimes helped loosen tongues. Taylor gave him a look; he cleared his throat and became completely professional.

"Lieutenant, Brandy served Mr. Stover last night. She said he was with another gentleman."

Taylor pulled a six-pack of photos she'd put together out of her jacket pocket and handed it to the waitress. "Do any of these men look familiar to you?"

Gustafson was on the top row, third photo.

Brandy didn't hesitate.

"That's the guy," she said, pointing to Gustafson.

"You're one-hundred-percent certain?"

"Absolutely. Gave me the creeps. He smiled too much. And didn't tip. They were going honky-tonking. The fat one asked me the best place to go. I sent them to Tootsies, of course, and suggested the Cadillac Ranch, too."

Taylor met Marcus's eye. "Thank you, ma'am. Please keep this to yourself. You may be called on again to provide information. Are you willing to do that?"

"I am. If he's a creep, I don't want him back in here. Hey, I gotta go. My manager's giving me the evil eye." She glanced coquettishly at Marcus. "Shout at me sometime."

Marcus blushed red, and Taylor gave him a smile.

"You're such a charmer."

"You know it. So this is our guy, huh?"

"Looks that way. You keep on this trail, see if you can nail down exactly what might have happened. I'm rather amazed, actually. Either this guy dropped his wallet while he was stabbing Go-Go, or she managed to slide it out of his pocket. Pretty incredible presence of mind for a girl who's stoned and dying."

"But she was an accomplished pickpocket. Maybe she targeted him just as he targeted her. And they both got screwed."

Taylor nodded. "That makes sense. Well done, Go-Go. She practically handed us her killer on a platter. I'm heading back to the office and hitting up the Internets."

"All right. See you later."

Taylor watched Marcus stride away, thankful to have his keen investigative mind at her disposal, then walked back to her vehicle. She had a date with a computer.

The email notification on her iPhone chimed just as she turned the engine over. It was Hagerman, from Fairfax County. According to him, there was no one named James Gustafson in the Virginia DMV system, and the address on the license was a vacant lot. Her killer was a ghost.

ViCAP, the Violent Criminal Apprehension Program, could be a homicide detective's best friend, if they knew exactly how to use it. It wasn't as easy as inputting your crime and the system spitting out a match to similar crimes. You had to know what to ask for. Taylor had unfortunately availed herself of its services many times in the past, and had the level of expertise needed to run the appropriate request chain into the queue. Hopefully the results would come back quickly, but the service wasn't fully automated. A real person had to do some of the legwork, and the FBI was backed up three ways to Sunday on requests. So she inputted the parameters, taking great care with the specifics of both Go-Go's and Heath Stover's murders—the exactness of the stab wounds, all the similarities she could find—crossed her fingers, and went on to the next component of her investigation: figuring out who this Gustafson man really was.

The ViCAP results came back several hours later, much quicker than she expected. She read the email in her inbox with trepidation, then sat back in her chair, let the realization wash over her. There were matches in the system from several places around the country, the most recent a homeless woman in New Orleans. Gustafson, whoever the son of a bitch really was, had been a busy, busy boy.

Taylor knew it was time to start raising the red flags. Too many jurisdictions, too many victims. She filled the chief in on her plan, got an *atta-girl*, then went to the source. Her fiancé was a profiler, after all.

Baldwin answered on the first ring. "Hey, love. How are you?"

"Hi, babe. I've been better. Two unsolved cases on my desk from yesterday alone, and just got a report back from ViCAP. I think I've got a serial on my hands." She gave him all the details, then emailed him the ViCAP report. She waited while he accessed it and read the findings. A few minutes later, he agreed.

"You might be right," he said. "What did you say this guy's name is again?"

"The license said James Gustafson, but Fairfax County just confirmed that no one by that name exists in the system, and the address is a fake. The license, the cards, all of it, they're either excellent identity theft or really sophisticated forgeries. Who is this guy?"

"An excellent question."

"My theory is he's been killing off the radar for years. And he broke his MO with this latest victim. He's been preying on homeless until now. Go-Go was a fuck up, she certainly looked the part, but hitting a well-established surgeon from New Orleans? One mistake could be an accident, sure, but the other . . . there's a tie to his past, I'm sure of it. The waitress got the impression they two men were friends, out for a night on the town. Maybe Stover knew the real identity of the killer, and Gustafson felt threatened."

"That's a solid theory. He killed a different type of victim out of sequence. The back-to-back kills, I'd bet he's in some sort of trouble and is decompensating."

"Well, he's screwed up. Now we know about him. He's on the radar, and I'm about to make his world hell."

"He sounds like someone who has spent his life being very, very careful. Listen, I'm totally wrapped up in this case, or else I'd help you myself. But I know who to call. I've worked with her on cases before. She's sharp. I think you should have a chat with her."

"What's her name?"

"Maggie O'Dell. Hold on a sec, let me get her number for you." He rattled off the numbers and she wrote them down.

"I'll call her right now. Thanks, honey. Call me later, okay?"

"Will do. Love you."

"Love you, too."

Taylor hung up the phone, waited a moment, then dialed. Even if O'Dell couldn't help, at least the FBI would be aware that something was hinky with the so-called James Robert Gustafson.

The call went to voicemail. Taylor left a message, told the agent who she was, her connection to Baldwin, that she had a significant ViCAP match and wanted to touch base. She hung up the phone, leaned back in her chair and put her boots on the desk.

She'd get some justice for Go-Go, and for Stover. Their deaths would not go unpunished. No matter what. And for the moment, that was the best she could do.

EPILOGUE

The lights of Washington D.C. greeted JR. Luminous, beautiful; the city was home. He always felt secure once he crossed into Fairfax County, knowing he was just miles from his basecamp. It had been a long trip, exhausting in its way, but so, so worth it.

Sated, he was calm again, the fury of the past month's excess slaking the thirst in his blood. Now he would lay low. Fit back into his life. Go to work like a good little boy. Recharge his batteries. Maybe a small vacation, somewhere in the mountains, where he could watch the snow fall, listen to birds chirp and water run and feel the cool air pass over his skin.

And remember. Always, always remember.

ABOUT THE STORY

BOOD SUGAR BABY is the middle part of a triad of stories that first appeared in SLICES OF NIGHT with my dear friends Erica Spindler and Alex Kava. To see where JR came from, and where he's headed next, I highly encourage you to purchase the full book, SLICES OF NIGHT.

NEW YORK TIMES BESTSELLING AUTHOR

J.T. ELLISON

"Everything a great crime
thriller should be."

—New York Times
bestselling author
Allison Brennan
on *All the Pretty Girls*

WHITEOUT

A TAYLOR JACKSON NOVELLA

"The wise man in the storm prays to God, not for safety from danger, but deliverance from fear."

– Ralph Waldo Emerson

1

October 9, 1987
Annecy, France
1900 Hours

My father's screams echo in the small car.

"*Monte, vite, vite. Angelie, baisse-toi! Baisse-toi!*"

My head hits the floor just as the window shatters. Blood, thick and hot, sprays my bare legs. I wedge myself under my mother's skirts, her thighs heavy against my shoulders. Somehow I know she is already dead. We are all dead.

Flashes of black.

Their voices, two distinctly male, one female. Another, a stranger's call, silenced abruptly with a short fusillade of bullets. The would-be savior's bicycle smashes into the side of our aging Peugeot. His body catapults across the hood onto the pavement beyond and his head hits the ground; the crack sounds like the opening of a cantaloupe, ripe and hard.

My father, his life leaving him, slides down in the seat like a puppet cut from its strings. He's whispering words over and over, faintly, and with the cacophony in the background I can barely hear him. I risk a glance, wishing I'd not. The image shall never leave me. Red, pulpy and viscous. He is missing half his face, but his full lips are moving.

"*Si toi survivre, cherchér ton Oncle Pierre. Je t'aime de tout mon cœur.*"

I hear nothing but the first words. Panic fills me. Though I recognize what is happening, the reality has just crept in.

Si toi survivre. If you survive.

I want to take his hand, to comfort him, to tell him I am there, that I, too, love him with all my heart. I reach for him as he dies. He shakes his head, trying to implore me to stay hidden, not to move. He isn't even speaking now, but I can hear his words in my head, like he has transferred his soul to my body for these last fluttering moments, has given himself up early to crowd into my body and try to save me.

Undeterred, my hand steals across the gearshift. I touch the cold skin of his thumb.

A roaring in my ears. There is pain beyond anything I've ever felt, and I go blank.

2

_____

October 8, 2013
Nashville, Tennessee
0415 Hours

Homicide never sleeps. At least that's what Taylor Jackson told herself when the phone roused her from a moderately deep slumber, the first decent shut-eye she'd had in a week. She'd finally crashed at 3:00 a.m., succumbing to the two-to-three hours she normally managed on a good night. The sheets were tangled around her legs, so she rolled to Baldwin's side of the bed, used a long arm to snake the phone off the hook.

"Who, what, where, when, and, most importantly, why?"

Homicide detective Lincoln Ross didn't miss a beat.

"Me. Your wake up call. Your phone. 4:15 a.m. Because you told me to get you up so you didn't miss your flight."

"You're fired."

"Excellent. I'll charter a plane to the Bahamas right now. See ya."

She yawned. "Okay, okay. I'm up. You downstairs?"

A faint horn sounded.

"On my way."

At least no one was dead. Not yet, anyway.

Jeans, boots, black cashmere T-shirt, leather jacket, ponytail, Carmex. Three minutes flat. Take that, Heidi Klum.

Two hours and three Diet Cokes later, her somewhat caffeinated body in an exit row window seat, the 737 rushed into the sky. She watched the ground fall away and asked herself again why she'd agreed to do this. The invitation had been the fault—*now, Taylor, be nice*—the *inspiration* of her fiancé, John Baldwin, whose place she was taking at the Freedom Conference, a small foreign intelligence initiative that met annually to hear about the latest tools for cyber intelligence and information gathering. The professional makeup of the conference was specific to clandestine services, but some civilian law enforcement officials attended as well. Baldwin had been set to speak about using behavioral profiling as a predictive analysis for terrorist attacks against the United States, and was featuring the case of the Pretender, a nasty serial killer who'd killed dozens in his bid to ruin all of their lives.

To ruin her life, as well.

Two years in the past, the moniker conjured chills and made her throat tighten.

Dead. He's dead. Stop it.

Baldwin had been called off at the last minute to deal with a skinner in Montana—what was it about these freaks who liked to remove their victims' skin?—and Taylor had agreed to take his place at the conference. She had his notes, his slideshow, though she was thinking of skipping that— there were crime scene photos from Nashville that showed her own bloodstains, and pools of her best friend's blood. She didn't know if she was quite ready to see them at all, not to mention plastered, bigger than life, on a presentation screen for an entire audience to see.

It had been interesting to see his analytical write-up about the case. It was so cut and dried. Like there were no other options. In Baldwin's world, everything that transpired was a foregone conclusion based on several psychological metrics. His evaluation made her feel better about what had happened. Taylor had lost her head. She'd hunted the man down, gone off grid in order to kill him, nearly lost her own life in the process, but in the end, it was Baldwin's finger that pulled the trigger.

He'd done that for her.

A foregone conclusion.

She settled deeper into the seat, shut her eyes. The least she could do was give his speech for him.

3

October 7, 2013
London, England
0000 Hours

T he phone in my flat bleats to life as I am leaving for the
airport.

My phone never rings, and this is purposeful. It is there
for emergencies: fires, break-ins, unanticipated scenarios that
could lead to my death. It is not for casual conversations, and
it never rings, because only one person has my number.

My heart speeds up, just a little. *Why is he calling?*
Why now?

I pick up the receiver. "*Oui?*"

"Angelie. What have you done?"

"*Je ne sais pas de quoi tu parles.*"

"In English, Angelie. How many times have I told you?"

"*Alors*, Pierre. Fine. I don't know what you're talking
about."

"Angelie, you know exactly what I'm talking about. A
couple of *gendârmes* just pulled Gregoire Campion's body out

of a duffel bag that was stashed in his bathtub. He was in pieces."

This news is both good and bad. Good, because the smug bastard is dead, at last. Bad, because if my Uncle Pierre is telling the truth and the body has been found so soon, the borders will be under extra scrutiny. Pierre has given me a gift without even knowing.

"That means nothing to me. I must go, *Oncle. À bientôt.*"

I hear his cry of protest as I drop the receiver. I must hurry.

From my closet I pull the necessary gear. A quick change of undergarments gives my thin body curves; tinted contacts turn my eyes blue; a beautifully made wig transforms me into an elegant blonde. I trade my jeans and trainers for a cashmere dress that clings perfectly to every inch of my altered body. A pair of knee-high leather Frye boots with specially made lifts adds a good three inches to my five-foot-four frame.

My name is now Alana Terbraak. I have been this woman before. Alana is fearless, a predator disguised as a Dutch-Canadian travel agent. She is the perfect cover for crossing borders; it is her job to scope out areas she sends her clients to. No one questions Alana's travel. She is one of my better identities.

I place several remaining identities in the bag, under a secure flap that is impossible to see with the naked eye, and pull the worn Canadian dollars from my safe. I mix them in with my Euros and pound notes, wipe down the small flat, lock everything up, and leave.

My plane departs in two hours, and I will not miss it.

4

October 8, 2013
Washington, D.C.
1400 Hours

An early snow greeted Taylor when she landed in D.C. As promised, a man was waiting for her by Baggage, holding an iPad; the screen spelled out her name. He took her bag silently and led her to a black sedan. Flakes danced around her, floating generously from an icy sky. She was glad for the warmth of the car.

When they were on the road, he offered her a drink. "There's bottled water, Scotch, and vodka in that cooler by your feet."

"Thank you." Taylor took a water. It was too early to drink, even though it might warm her from the inside out.

The snow continued to cascade down as they drove to the west, getting heavier the closer they got to the Chesapeake Bay. Charles, the driver, slowed, taking it easy; the roads were getting slick.

Taylor gave up, turned up the heat in the backseat. "Too

bad you don't have hot chocolate in here. I didn't know snow was in the forecast."

"It wasn't. We've got an Alberta Clipper that snuck up on us, same storm that's wreaking havoc back in the Midwest and down in Florida. It's a good thing you flew in today. Tomorrow you'd be stuck at the airport, shivering your skinny self off. Gonna get bad, that's what they're saying. Big blizzard, storm surge up the bay, power lines down from the ice. Hope you brought a sweater."

"I did. My friend Maggie O'Dell—she's an FBI agent— called last night and warned me that the storm was going to be bad. When Maggie speaks, I listen."

Forty minutes and several white-knuckled slips and slides later, Charles deposited her at the front steps of the Old Maryland Resort and Spa. "I'll bring up your bag. You're to meet the conference folk at the desk."

"Thanks, Charles. And thanks for getting me here in one piece." Taylor tried to hand him a tip, but he brushed it off with a shy smile. She shivered in her leather jacket and mounted the stairs to the resort's reception area. A woman waved at her the moment she walked in the door. She was small to the point of being elfin, gray hair cut into a chic chin-length bob, cornflower blue eyes, and a friendly smile. Taylor felt a bit like a linebacker on her approach.

"Welcome to Maryland, Lieutenant Jackson. I'm Cherry Gregg, the chair of the Freedom Conference. We are so glad to have you here. Was the ride from the airport okay?"

"It was great, thank you. I appreciate you sending a car for me." That was a lie; Taylor had wanted to rent a car, not liking the idea of being stuck an hour out of D.C. on the Chesapeake Bay without her own transportation, but it was all part of the speaker gig—getting coddled and treated like royalty. Samantha Owens, her best friend, lived in Georgetown, and was planning to come down at the end of the weekend and ferry Taylor back to D.C. for a night of catch-up. She could live for two days without a car, especially because the conference was being held at a lavish spa resort that seemed to have every amenity she might need.

"If you're anything like me, you hate not having your own car, but we are at your service this weekend. Anyplace you'd like to go, just call down to the desk, and your driver will ferry you about like a queen."

Taylor didn't even bother trying to hide her surprise. "You read my mind. How did you know?"

Gregg answered with a slight laugh. "Lieutenant, I was a CIA field agent for twenty years, and COS—sorry, Chief of Station—in four different countries. Reliable transportation was always my number-one priority. If you get completely desperate, there's an Enterprise car rental four blocks south."

Taylor laughed, liking Gregg immediately. "I'll remember that. Is the weather going to hold up?"

"It's not. Thankfully, you're the last one to arrive. We've got everyone else safely here already. We're told they have back up generators and enough fuel to hold us for at least a week, should we be so unlucky as to lose power, and the kitchens are fully stocked. There are fireplaces in many of the rooms with plenty of wood, too. One of the treats of this place, and it's going to work in our favor this weekend."

"Sounds like they thought of everything."

"Oh, they did, I assure you. Most importantly, the bar is prepped and ready, too. They laid in an extra ration of grog for us all."

"Priorities. I like it."

"You bet. I'm so happy you could join us, Lieutenant. You're very kind to take over Dr. Baldwin's spot. Would you like to settle into your room, then meet me back here in two hours? We've got a cocktail reception we'd like you to attend —it's business dress. We'll get you introduced to the other panelists, and there's a fair amount of people who'd like to meet you. Your story, your history . . . well, let's just say folks are interested."

Folks were always interested. Taylor attracted trouble like dust on black furniture. Inevitable.

"I don't know if that's good or bad, but you're too kind. Thank you."

"Here's your key—you're up on the fifth floor, in the Maryland Suite. I've been told they used to call it the Crab Cake Suite, but people complained."

They shared another laugh, and Taylor set off for the elevators. The room was at the end of a long, narrow hallway. She held her pass to the door, and it unlocked.

Her first impression was a blizzard of white—white walls, white furniture, white bedding, white carpeting. The cleaning bills must be astronomical. There was a fireplace at the far end of the suite, and the bathroom walls were clear glass, with a hot tub that had a perfect view of the fire.

She started to giggle, took a picture and texted it, then dialed Baldwin's cell. He answered on the first ring.

"I would suggest you plan to drink champagne instead of red wine."

"I know, right? The picture doesn't do it justice." She went to the windows, pulled back the heavy curtains. "Baldwin, you should see this place. The view of the Chesapeake Bay is spectacular, or would be in the summer—right now it's just snowing. But you saw that hot tub and fireplace. It's like the sex bomb suite or something."

"Sounds more like a honeymoon suite. I'm sorry I have to miss it." There was a note in his voice that made her stomach hitch.

"I'm sorry too. Though I am wondering why, exactly, they reserved this particular room for *you*."

"I'd told them you were coming," he replied.

She started to laugh then, and he joined her.

"You're naughty. Everything moving along with your skinner?"

"Don't tell anyone, but we're serving a warrant in an hour. I think we've nailed the psycho."

"That's my guy. Always gets his man. Good job."

"Thanks, hon. Just glad to get another monster off the streets. Listen, there's a really bad storm heading your way. So stay inside, stay warm and dry, and if you get stuck there, I'll come and rescue you. And we can see what the real view is from that hot tub. Okay?"

"Sounds wonderful. Love you. Bye."

She unpacked her suitcase. Business casual for the cocktail party—she guessed jeans wouldn't work. She pulled a black wool skirt from the bag, and switched her motorcycle boots for knee-high cognac leather. A black cashmere sweater set and her grandmother's pearls completed the outfit. She glanced in the mirror.

"You look entirely too respectable." She took her hair down, let it hang loose around her shoulders.

"Better. Much less uptight."

And the woman in the mirror grinned back.

5

Chesapeake Bay, Maryland
1700 Hours

Taylor allowed herself a second glass of wine. The cocktail party was in full swing, the stories flying fast and furious. After the initial round of introductions, and a few awkward questions answered blithely, she'd stuck to listening, watching. There was a beautiful brunette built like a brick shithouse across the way who'd garnered the attention of practically every man in the place. She had a wonderfully exotic accent, a loud voice, and was telling stories about Sudan's second civil war in the '80s. Something about Gaddafi switching sides to support Mengistu, and a microfiche that she'd planted to thwart a southern attack.

" . . . But he never thought to look in the lid of the teapot, and believe you me, I've never looked at cinnamon tea the same way again," and the crowd roared with appreciative laughter.

Taylor smiled to herself and crossed the room to watch the storm. Snow on water fascinated her. Nashville wasn't a bastion of winter weather; it just got cold, and rarely snowed more than an inch or two. This was a full-fledged blizzard, and it was monstrously beautiful.

"Intelligence officers. We're like bees: we can only speak in one language, and if you don't know it, there's no manual for translation."

Taylor turned to see the man who'd spoken. He was in his late fifties, small and dapper, with short gray hair and a sad smile, and the barest hint of an accent. French, she thought, though it was very refined.

"Oh, we cops are the same way. Our stories are usually bloodier, though."

"Give them time. A few more pops, and they'll be into Afghanistan. Plenty of bloody stories there. I'm Thierry Florian. I know your fiancé. He's a good man. We worked together in Argentina last year."

"Ah, Argentina. So that's where he was. I knew it was South America, but Baldwin is always very careful not to disclose too much of his . . . private work."

"Nature of the beast. Helps to have a spouse in the business. No awkward questions at two in the morning."

"We're not married. Yet."

"There's time." His head was cocked to the side like a spaniel. "Your photos don't do you justice. Your eyes are different colors. Your right is darker than your left. I've never seen heterochromia with gray like that. *C'est trés jolie.* Very pretty."

He wasn't hitting on her, just noticing. It still felt weird, so she changed the subject. "Are you still clandestine service then, Thierry?"

"I retired from the DGSE in November after thirty years in. I run the Macallan Group now. Do you know who we are?"

"I know you're not a bunch of Scotch enthusiasts."

He laughed. "That's right. We grew out of the Futures

Working Group, but we are a privately held company. Very dedicated, and very much off book." He winked.

"Baldwin's told me about your work. You've assembled an interesting gang of people."

"We have people from every section, multiple countries. From CIA to Mossad and military to police. We even have a couple of novelists, brilliant men and women whose sole purpose is to dream up the most unfathomable situations for us to scrutinize, because real life always imitates art."

"Doesn't it though."

His shoulders shrugged, a perfectly Gallic gesture Taylor had never seen an American man master. "*Oui.* It is strange, life. Any time you want to join us, say the word. You have just the right temperament to fit in. I was hoping to discuss it with you this weekend."

Taylor raised her eyebrows. "What, you want me to come to a meeting or something?"

She envisioned pipes and dark smoky rooms, green computer screens and cables spitting out from teletype machines. Romantic thoughts of spies long past—which was silly, because she'd seen Baldwin at work, and it wasn't cool and dreamy. It was brutal, and watching him in that element always gave her a chill down the spine. When he shut down his compassion, his became another person entirely.

Florian gave a small laugh. "So to speak. The meeting in question would be of a more permanent nature."

"Oh. Are you offering me a job?"

"I am. I would like to hook Baldwin, too. He understands our mission, that our work is vital to the safety of all of our countries. Like the intelligence services, we collect and analyze data, only act when necessary. We share with many of them if we see they are behind the curve ball."

Act when necessary. Again, she was getting into a shadow world she didn't like to think of. Some would see it as breaking the law, something she was vehemently opposed to. But for the greater good, as Baldwin always liked to point out —for the greater good, rules were sometimes meant to be bent and broken. And if it saved lives? Absolutely.

"I think you mean behind the eight ball."

"*Alors*, my English. Yes. The eight ball. But more importantly, we use the information we collect to anticipate. Anticipate, and avoid. The problem with the FBI, with your police forces, with law enforcement, in general, is the very nature of the work. React, react, react. The CIA is better, but even they are stymied by their political ties. Black ops hardly exist anymore. There is no funding for special programs, and no balls on your politicians.

"Our work is entirely independent and very proactive. We want to prevent the attacks before they start, rather than hunt down the perpetrators after the fact. You talk John Baldwin into coming along, and you can name your price. You are both worth it."

"That's very kind, but it's not about the money—"

"Of course not. You are, I believe the right word is, an idealist. You fight for justice, because ever fiber of your being screams that it is the right thing to do. Just think, Taylor Jackson, what power there would be in *preventing* the attacks you investigate, *before* they occur. That is our job. And your unique abilities are worth a great deal to me.

"You both come from money; you have also earned enough to retire comfortably. So think of this salary as a cushion. You can buy his-and-hers Ferraris, or give it away to starving African children, I do not care. I need your minds. You are instinctive, and smart, and you could do a lot of good for your country. Think about it. *Santé*."

He clinked her glass and walked away.

She took a sip of wine to cover her discomfiture. *Well. That was interesting.*

She dismissed the conversation. She was perfectly happy working homicide for Metro Nashville. She didn't like change. She especially didn't like the idea of abandoning her team.

And preventing murder? Preventing attacks? No one could do that, not effectively. Someone evil would always slip through the cracks.

The snow was heavier than ever, coming down so hard she could barely see the lights of the cars passing by on the street below. She checked her phone; the forecast was now calling for twenty inches. A small bloom of panic started in her chest. The last time she'd been snowed in, a blizzard of epic proportions in Scotland, not-so-great things had happened.

Florian caught her eye from across the room and smiled politely. He was clearly watching her, and she resented it, though she didn't know why. He'd made an offer. She'd gotten them before. It was what it was.

But. . . .

She'd be forty in a few years, and as far as her career was concerned, she would need to make a decision about her role going forward. It was already being whispered that she'd make Captain soon, would be in charge of Nashville's entire Criminal Investigative Division, and that meant she'd be off the streets and on to the paperwork and political glad-handing. Captain Jackson. A few more years, then further up the brass ladder. Maybe even Chief in ten years. More bureaucratic nonsense. And then what? Run for office? No, thank you. She had too many opinions and not enough reserve to stop her from sharing them freely.

Baldwin wanted her to join the FBI, which would be a logical step. And though she admired everything he did, she knew she wouldn't fit in. The culture was too restrictive. She had enough bossing around at Metro that drove her mad.

Having to follow the kind of dictates that the federal govern-ment imposed on law enforcement was a recipe for disaster.

The Macallan Group. Proactive rather than reactive. Huh.

She looked around the room again for Thierry Florian, but didn't see him. She sent him a mental *thanks a lot*. There would be no sleep for her tonight.

6

October 9
Chesapeake Bay, Maryland
0000 Hours

The cameras are on for my safety. I made sure before we began. They will catch everything. Just in case.

The kisses are going a mile a minute. Our clothes are gone, my slip is rucked up over my hips. I skipped panties, hopeful for this moment. It makes things so much easier. His hands rush over my body, grasping my skin, kneading my buttocks, hands hurrying to my thighs and then my back, up and down and around, and I whisper, "Too fast, too fast."

He slows, smiling, his right palm lingering along the curve of my hip, then sliding to my breast, his mouth featherweight, following his touch.

Better.

It has been too long. I should stop him before it goes much further, but it feels so good to be touched, to be loved.

His hand slips down between my thighs, and a moan escapes my lips. *Stay in control, stay in control*, but I am losing it. He is too good, too skilled, and I hit the point where I don't care anymore. I am just an animal, needing, wanting. His finger is deep inside me, and we are still standing, skin-to-skin, glued together. And it feels so good.

Fuck it. I inch up, and he catches the movement, effortlessly lifts me, and my legs wrap around his waist. He is breathing hard, ready to go. Pushing against me. Waves of pleasure shudder through me. I think I might faint, take a deep breath to clear my head.

He catches my lips, kissing, sucking, staring into my eyes. He moves his hand, and I can't help but respond.

Recognizing it is time, he lays me down on the bed and slows his movement further, stroking, caressing, gentling when I want it rough, the mistake of a new lover. "Now," I urge, and he smiles and spreads my legs wide, one palm on the inside of each thigh, and thrusts into me, hard. I cry out, go right over the edge into the bliss, and he comes with me.

I lose time; I always do after sex. Hazardous, but inescapable. Hence the cameras. An old habit, hard to break.

When our breathing slows, he rolls off me, to the side, and I rise from the bed.

"Don't get up," he says, leaning on an elbow, beckoning me back.

Too late. I am already at my purse, the bag open, the cold steel in my hand. My favorite companion, the only one I truly trust. I turn to him, a brief smile playing on my lips.

"Thank you," I say, and fire. The suppressed round sounds like a sigh in the darkened room. It takes him between the eyes, and he collapses back onto the bed.

Another means to an end.

I replace the weapon, dress, brush my hair, enjoy the flush of color on my cheeks. I wipe down the room, grab my cell phone, turn off the video camera. Face the connecting door to the room next to my newly dead lover.

A moment twenty-five years in the making. Finally here.

I jimmy the lock, silent as possible. The door opens, and there he is. Asleep, quiet. Far from innocent. He looks older in his sleep.

Older, and soon to be very, very dead.

7

0110 Hours

Taylor showered and changed, then stalked around her suite, wishing for something to do. No pool table, as the bar was closed for the night. Baldwin was getting some well-earned sleep, having made a successful arrest. She'd forgotten to pack a book, though there was probably a library on the hotel grounds.

Truth be told, nothing would distract her enough. She was worried about the storm. The gathering winds were howling past her window; a small piece of siding had come loose and was rattling. She could just make out people moving around outside—workers, most likely, sent out into the storm to batten down the hatches. They worked in twos, probably tied together so they wouldn't get lost.

A scene from a Laura Ingalls Wilder book pranced into her head, something she'd not thought about since she was a child. The rope between the shed and the house, followed to feed the animals, so Pa wouldn't get lost. Or Laura. She couldn't remember exactly who was meant to be saved by the slender thread, but it had worked, and all ended well.

She had no tether to keep her safe, and it worried her.

The television gave no succor, either. The whole country seemed to be in the grip of this massive and mercurial storm. The Weather Channel was covering the huge, multi-state event causing chaos across the country. The mega-storm had swooped down from Canada, slicing through Illinois, where Rockford had received record-breaking snow totals, and people were still lost, stuck on highways and in houses inaccessible to rescue crews. She sent her friend Mary Catherine Riggio a text, checking on her, knowing the Rockford P.D. homicide detective would be out helping the emergency prep folks, but didn't hear back. And poor Maggie was down in Pensacola, Florida, which was flooded out after twenty inches of rain, and still experiencing thunderstorms and high winds. Major damage. The radar clearly showed the catastrophic storm heading right toward the Washington, D.C., area, which meant Taylor was now directly in its path.

The Weather Channel's anchor warned everyone to hunker down, because it was going to get worse before it got better. The snow totals were going to break records all up the Eastern seaboard, the storm surges would cause widespread flooding up and down the Chesapeake Bay.

Great.

As a first responder herself, Taylor wasn't used to sitting in a hotel room waiting for a storm to hit. If this were Nashville, she'd be in the command center at Metro, giving instructions, helping the city cover all the quadrants to minimize the danger to its citizens. She gave a moment's thought to calling the Calvert County Sheriff, offering her services, but realized she'd be as wanted as a wart.

She lit the fire, grabbed a beer from the mini-fridge, snuggled into the bed, and watched the flames dance while she listened to the warnings. When she could take no more, she flipped off The Weather Channel, found *The Princess Bride* on one of the movie channels, and turned down the lights. She knew the words practically by heart, but it was better than nothing.

The R.O.U.S., Rodents of Unusual Size, were beginning to lurk when the power went off.

The fireplace was down to coals as well. She'd burned through more logs than she'd realized, and the stash was getting low.

Taylor picked up the room phone, heard nothing. She pressed a few buttons, but no dial tone started. Thankfully, she'd thought to charge her cell phone. She called down to the front desk. Nothing. The lines were dead.

She knew the hotel had generators, she just needed them to kick in. It would get cold in the room quickly—the fireplace didn't put off that much heat—so she grabbed the extra blanket from the armoire and tossed it on the end of the bed.

Nothing to do but wait, and try to sleep. After an hour of tossing and turning, she managed to drift, her rest disturbed by terrible dreams. She was cold, so cold, hiking through the snow, with no one in sight, just the expanse of white spreading in all directions. She knew it was the end; she wouldn't survive. And the voice of the Pretender whispered in her ear.

_____

8

0200 Hours

I t was two in the morning when the fire alarms went off. She scrambled from the bed, shaking off the chill, not sure if it was the temperature or the dreams, and threw on her jeans. It was cold in the room, her fingers fumbled with the buttons. After shrugging into her jacket, she pocketed her cell and wallet, and opened the door to the hallway with care. She could smell smoke.

Other guests were streaming from their rooms. Her hand went absently to her waist, reaching for the comfort of her Glock. Nothing there. She hesitated for a fraction of a second. Better safe than sorry.

She went back into her room, made sure the door was latched, then retrieved her Glock 27 from its case in the interior of her suitcase. The key to the lock shook in her hands—damn, it was cold. She had only brought the small backup gun, certainly hadn't planned to get it from its case. She hadn't expected to need it, not at a conference in a swanky hotel.

She slapped a magazine in place, put two more in her jacket pocket, and stowed the weapon in a small belt-clipped holster. She felt sure she wouldn't be the only one armed out of this crew—cops and counterintelligence officers weren't that different.

More comfortable with the familiar weight on her hip, she left the room, followed the remaining stragglers to the stairwell.

"What's the matter?" she called out to the nearest man.

"Dunno," he replied. "Guess it's a fire. Wish they'd turn that bloody alarm off though, it's breaking my eardrums."

"No kidding. It's deafening."

Down the five flights, carefully picking their way, with cell phones giving the only decent light. There was emergency lighting on the walls, but the lights were dim, as if they weren't getting proper connections.

The stairwell exited into the lobby. A crowd of people had gathered in the dark. They weren't being evacuated, just left to mingle in the cavernous space.

Taylor didn't like this at all. She bumbled around in the dark a bit, saw Cherry, her face underlit by a flashlight, making her seem like a ghoul. She was pale and carrying a clipboard. Just as Taylor reached her, the alarm stopped, leaving her ears ringing.

Cherry gave her a wan smile. "Oh, good, Lieutenant Jackson. I can mark you off the list."

"What's going on? Is there a fire?"

"When the power went out, the generators to the rooms failed. A small fire started on the roof, and they're trying to contain it. There's a skeleton staff on the night shift, plus several people couldn't—or wouldn't—make the drive in, and the roads are blocked now, so the fire trucks can't get here. They're doing the best they can."

"Should we be evacuating people?"

"No, not yet. Thankfully, the lobby is on a separate generator, and the heat will stay on in here for a while. As soon as they give the word, we can send people back to their rooms. Might as well settle in until they give the all clear."

"You need to put me to work, I'm going bonkers. What can I do to help?"

Cherry flashed the light on her list. "We're still missing a few people. Would you be willing to take a flashlight and hike back upstairs, knock on doors? Be very careful, we wouldn't want you getting hurt."

"Absolutely. Who are we missing?"

"Let's see . . . Ellis Stamper—he's in 4880. And Thierry Florian, right next door in 4900. Hildy Rochelle, as well, the brunette woman who was charming everyone tonight. She's on the fifth floor, 5380."

The man nearest them said, "Cherry, I saw her earlier. She's down here somewhere."

"Oh, good. Thanks for letting me know, Ron." She turned back to Taylor. "Just the two gentlemen, then."

"Got it. On my way."

"Thank you, Taylor. I appreciate it."

Cherry handed Taylor an extra flashlight. She headed back to the stairwell.

Now that it was silent and empty, Taylor had to admit it was a little creepy. She climbed the stairs, enjoying the burn in her thighs that started on the third floor. It warmed her up. The faint scent of smoke was stronger up here, but no worse than when she'd exited her room.

The fourth floor was deserted. Taylor turned on the flashlight—it was amazing how dark the hallway had become. She heard nothing but the whistling wind.

Room 4880 was halfway down the hall. She knocked on the door.

"Excuse me, Mr. Stamper? You're needed downstairs."

Nothing.

She banged a few more times. He must have passed her in the night. She walked down to the room next door. "Mr. Florian, it's Taylor Jackson. The generators are out to the rooms, and there's a fire on the roof. They want everyone downstairs. Cherry sent me up to find you."

Silence again.

They must have already made their way down. A wasted trip.

She'd just started back toward the stairwell when she heard the noise.

She stopped dead in her tracks, listened for it. Yes, there it was again. It sounded like crying. She pulled open the stairwell door and let it slam closed, then stepped lightly back to the two men's rooms.

Stamper's room was still dead quiet, but she could swear there were hushed voices coming from Florian's.

She knocked again. "Mr. Florian? Are you in there?"

Nothing. The silence was pervasive, complete. False alarm?

She shook it off. Must have been the wind. Or, better yet, this old place was probably haunted, and she'd just been tricked by a ghost.

Not that she believed in ghosts.

Not really.

She went for the stairwell, made her way back down to the lobby. She found Cherry in the spot she'd left her.

"Nobody home. They must already be down here, and you just missed them."

Cherry's brow creased.

"They're not here, Taylor. I've talked to everyone, they are all in the room behind the lobby's entrance. There's a giant wood-burning fireplace in there, and plenty of logs. They've opened the bar, there's some water boiling for tea and hot chocolate. But everyone who went in passed by me, and I didn't see them."

"Well, that is weird. Let's go do a lap, see if they came late."

It took five minutes of flashing lights in strangers' eyes to see that there was no trace of either man.

9

0230 Hours

Too close. Surely the woman won't come back, she will assume the bastard has already vacated his room.

I remember seeing her at the cocktail party, tall, blond, aloof. Looked frigid as hell. Pretty, if you liked the ice princess type. She gave off a whiff of danger, her eyes watching every move in the room. A cop, for sure. I've seen too many in my day not to be able to pick them from the crowd.

Florian is whimpering again. I kick him in the ribs. "Shut up, old man. We are not finished."

He is missing part of a finger, a play I wasn't planning to have to employ so early in our friendly chat. But he was not taking me seriously, so I had to make a point. It was the tip of his pinky, just a quick snip of the shears, but bloody, for all that.

I flash the light in his eyes, his pupils hurriedly shrink. He moans again.

"I will take the gag out if you promise to cooperate. To tell me what I want to know."

A nod.

"If you don't cooperate, there will be more fingers. Then toes, and hands, followed by your feet. *Tu comprends*? Do you understand?"

Another nod. I swear his skin pales—perhaps I've finally made my point.

I remove the gag, dragging it down over his chin. He gulps for air. "They will come back. You can't get away with this."

"How disappointing. *Crétin. Maudite vache.* Do you not know who I am?"

He looks, uncomprehending. He does not know me in the darkness, in his confusion. Granted, I'm still in the brown wig from earlier, the dark contacts. A small adjustment to my nose.

I pull the wig from my head, and he gasps.

But it is not in recognition, it is in pain. He has passed out. I forget his age. He will not last the night at this rate. I must slow down.

His words penetrate. *They will come back.*

They will. I should move him. But where?

My finger taps against my thigh, and I hear his intake of breath. He is awake, and recognizes that small movement. Finally, he knows who he is dealing with.

"*Mon dieu.* Angelie. Angelie Delacroix. Is that you?"

"*Oui, Thierry. C'est moi. Je suis vivant, et tu êtes mort.*"

The knife slides into his ribs with ease, just above the kidneys. Not deep enough to be fatal. Not yet.

I whisper in his ear, the words harsh, metallic on my tongue. The question I've been waiting two and a half decades to ask.

"Why did you kill my father?"

10

Unintended consequences. The fire was contained, and everyone was given the okay to go back to their rooms. But without power, the electronic key cards wouldn't work. The generator that powered the rooms was damaged in the fire. Until the power was restored, they were stuck. The hotel staff was forced to gather everyone back in the lobby near the fireplace.

The generator to the first floor lobby ran out of fuel just after 4:00 a.m.

The depth of the snow was overwhelming. In just eight hours, there were at least four feet pushing up against the hotel's front door, and it was still coming down. Ice crackled along the windows, the moaning wind fighting to gain entry into the hotel. Cracks sounded in the distance, tree limbs collapsing under the sudden weight.

There was talk of evacuation, but Taylor knew that was a pipe dream—what were they going to do, bring a bus in? And where would they go? The entire eastern seaboard was caught in the grip of the storm. Nothing was moving. They were stuck here.

Cherry was waiting for a maintenance man to arrive with an override master key that would allow them access to rooms 4880 and 4900. She paced the lobby, staring out into the snow. Taylor figured she knew deep down there was no help coming.

Everyone knew something was wrong, that Thierry Florian and Ellis Stamper were missing. Whether they were in their rooms, or had left the premises and weren't able to return, no one knew. The idea of the two men caught out in that blizzard was unthinkable.

Stamper, it turned out, was also a member of the Macallan Group. He was Thierry's assistant, though that term was a misnomer. *Right-hand* would be more appropriate. *Bodyguard* might even come into play.

Their relationship had even been speculated about once or twice, though Florian put those vulgar rumors to rest quite openly, taking a beautiful young lover who'd ended up as his wife three years earlier. Stamper had married a year later as well.

It was their habit to get two-bedroom suites at hotels, ostensibly so Stamper could watch out over his boss. But for this event, the suites were booked, and they'd been forced into adjoining rooms instead. The front desk clerk remembered their conversation clearly, and the manager had sent a fruit basket to Mr. Florian to apologize for the mix-up.

There was no way to call either wife, to ask if she'd heard from her husband. No power, no cell service, no landlines. They were an island, in the dark and cold.

Taylor was chomping at the bit to get into the rooms. She wasn't in her jurisdiction, or she'd be ordering people around. Instead, the hotel staff was waiting for a representative from the Sheriff's office to show up before they opened the doors.

Precious moments ticking away. Modern technology was fantastic until the world was plunged into the dark, and then the Middle Ages again reigned supreme.

Taylor watched the minutes pass on her TAG Heuer watch, catching Cherry's eye every once in a while.

It took people who'd become accustomed to death to sense that this situation was very, very bad.

11

0500 Hours

"Angelie. You must know, I did everything in my power to stop the murder. Your father, he would not listen. We begged him to stay put in Paris, that we had him covered, but he loaded up your mother and sister and you into the caravan and drove south. He thought he could protect you better than I. He was wrong."

"He was not wrong. He died protecting us. It was your job to keep him safe, to keep us all safe. He stole secrets for you, and you let him be gunned down. They killed my sister first, did you know that? Beatrice was six. Six, Florian—dead in my mother's lap. Her blood dripping into my hair."

"Is that what you're doing, Angelie? Systematically murdering all of the people involved in your father's case? Yes, I heard tonight about poor Gregoire Campion. I didn't realize you were capable of such an atrocity. You cut him into pieces and stowed his body in a duffel in his bathtub. The man was your friend, Angelie. How could you do that to him?"

I laugh. "A friend? Campion was never my friend. He used me, for years. Like all of you. His death is not on my conscience, Thierry. I did simply what I must to gain the truth, at last."

"*Alors*, Angelie, this is a pointless exercise. Murdering the minders will not bring your father back. It will not bring your family back. We did everything we could to protect them. In the end, the cause was simple. Your father trusted the wrong people."

Fury crowds into my chest. This is the lie Campion spewed when he was at the end. I slap Florian's face, hard.

"Lies. Don't even try to justify yourself. Oncle Pierre has shared the file with me, Thierry. I know exactly what happened. I know how you sold my father out to the Iraqis. He was the only one who had the capability to help them build their bloody bombs, and you told them where he would be that day."

His voice is soft in the darkness. "No, Angelie. That is wrong. We would never give your father to them. Never."

Florian goes silent. Something is not right here, I can feel it. I take a lap around the dark room, trying and failing to gather my temper. The cover-up is secure; all involved have the same story. How to get the truth? What will I have to do to this master of spies to find the answers I seek?

"Angelie. You've served your country admirably for fifteen years. You're one of the best assets we've ever had. Your future is bright. Why are you doing this? Why now, after all these years?"

I pull the crumbled paper from my purse. So many lives, so many sacrifices, all to procure this single sheet of paper.

I put it in front of his face, play a flashlight over the words.

He reads, then chews on his lip before he calmly sits back on the floor.

"Don't do this," he says, and there is no pleading in his

voice, not like the others, who begged for their lives. Florian won't beg. He will find a way to go down swinging. He taught me that, at least.

I can't keep the tears from my voice. "I know, Thierry. I know it all."

12

0600 Hours

T he skies outside were dark gray. No power yet, but it wasn't the dead-of-night blackness from earlier. The mood in the room lightened, especially when the staff began handing out apples and bananas and granola bars, and stoked up the fire. If they just had some marshmallows, this would be more like a damn camping trip.

Taylor looked at her watch for the millionth time. "It's nearly six, Cherry. There's no more time to waste. It's been too long."

Cherry had dark circles below her eyes. She was clearly exhausted. But she came to life at Taylor's words, almost in relief. "I agree. I'm worried sick. Let's get the manager on duty, find out what the hell is happening."

At her wave, the hotel's manager on duty, a burly man named Fred, approached.

"Ma'am? Bad news. Our mechanic isn't going to make it. The Sheriff's office is responding to a huge wreck—buncha cars on the highway crashed, they can't spare anyone for at least an hour. We're stuck, I'm afraid."

"Fred, I'm sorry, but we need in those rooms. The Freedom Conference will pay for the damages we're about to incur."

"What?"

Taylor chimed in. "Can you let us into your maintenance room? We're going to need some tools. A wrench and a screwdriver, for starters. A crowbar, if you have it."

Fred's brown creased. "Um, ma'am, just what are you planning to do?"

Taylor smiled. "Easy. Bust the locks off the doors."

"I can't let you do that. Those locks cost—"

"It doesn't matter. There could be two lives at stake in there, and we're not going to wait any longer."

"I gotta talk to the main hotel property managers, they're in Denver. They own the resort. I can't let you—"

Taylor got in his face, her voice stern. "Fred, we aren't going to wait. We will take responsibility. I'm a cop. You place the blame squarely on my head, and I'll cover your back. The tools, now."

People always backed down when she used that tone. Fred grabbed a flashlight, and, without a word, headed toward the back stairs.

"I've got this, Cherry. I'll be back for you in a minute."

It took five minutes to gather the tools she thought she'd need. Fred wasn't talking, just shined the big industrial flashlight where Taylor asked. She'd scared him enough that he was keeping his mouth shut; she assumed he probably had a record he hadn't disclosed, something minor, and didn't want his bosses getting wind of his issues. She met guys like him in her investigations all the time. DUIs, late on their child support, warrants for traffic violations, gambling debts. Stupid stuff that should just be handled. Instead, they furtively tried to hide their misdeeds.

"Let's go up. I might need your muscle," she said, and Fred sullenly shined the light on the stairs for her. When they reached the first floor lobby, he stopped cold.

"You know what? You're on your own from here. I ain't going up there. I'm not going to be held responsible for this."

Of course not.

"A noble speech, Fred. Thanks for doing the right thing."

She left him gaping after her and found Cherry warming her hands near the fireplace. "I've got everything. Are you ready?"

"Yes," she said simply, and fell in line behind Taylor. The whispers started as they left the room.

As they climbed the stairs, the wind shrieked harder around the building, and its violent passage heightened the echoes of their footfalls in the darkened stairwell. It was even creepier than last night—Taylor sensed the storm was peaking. Hopefully, this would be the worst of it.

The fourth floor was eerily quiet. Once the stairwell door was shut, the wind's fury was muffled a bit.

The two women walked quickly down the hall. They stopped at Stamper's room first.

Taylor didn't move for a moment, just breathed deeply. All the hair stood up on the back of her neck. Something was different. Something was wrong.

"Do you smell that?"

Cherry nodded. She'd been around enough destruction, enough death, to recognize the scent.

"Blood," she whispered.

Taylor nodded. This wasn't going to end well, she could just feel it.

She took the crowbar to the door, not caring about the damage she was inflicting. With a great wrenching groan, the lock pulled free of the door. The metal warped, and Taylor used the screwdriver to wedge the tongue out of the bolt. It still didn't free, so she gave it a strong kick, and the door latch popped free.

She drew her weapon, took a flashlight from Cherry, and cross-armed the light under her shooting hand, the outside corners of each wrist meeting in a kiss.

The room was dark, the curtains pulled closed. Taylor swung the light around the room until she saw the body. The coppery tang of blood, a scent Taylor was much too familiar with, grew stronger the nearer she got to the bed.

Their worst fears, confirmed.

Cherry gasped aloud when she saw the neat hole in Ellis Stamper's forehead. The greatest damage was to the back of his skull, which had a massive hole in it where the bullet exited.

"Jesus. He's been executed."

Taylor said nothing, just moved the flashlight around the room, taking in the scene. He was naked on the bed, the sheets twisted. Underlying the blood was the scent of musk. Taylor approached the body, shined her flashlight up and down the length of him. There was a spent condom in the trashcan next to the bed.

"He had company."

Cherry joined her. "Conference sex. Happens all the time. We should make sure this doesn't get back to his wife." She reached for the condom; Taylor stopped her.

"What are you doing? We don't touch anything. If you persist I'll escort you from the room. Do you understand?"

Cherry gave Taylor a sad little smile. "I was COS for twenty years. My first responsibility is to my people."

"Not to the law, not to justice? You're willing to cover this up? Whoever he screwed most likely killed him."

"This will ruin him. His family, his honor—"

"Cherry, the man's dead. I daresay he's already ruined. Let's worry about soothing hurt feelings if the time comes. There's DNA on that condom, a piece of the puzzle we can't pretend doesn't exist. Get it?"

"Cops. Always afraid to do the right thing." There was a note of exasperated humor in Cherry's voice, which was a good thing, but Taylor gave her a baleful eye anyway, and she moved away from the bed.

The flashlight pummeled the darkness once more, and Taylor spied the connecting door to the next room. She thought about the room set up, realized it went to 4900.

"Cherry, look. This goes into Florian's room. Easier to get through this than tearing the electronic lock off the other door."

"I agree. But Taylor, be careful."

"*Careful* is my middle name."

Taylor eased the door open with her shoulder; it wasn't locked, or fully closed. Unlocked she could understand; if Stamper was Florian's bodyguard, he would need access to the room. And if the rumors were true, and they *were* lovers? That logic was sound; the used condom spoke volumes. Could Florian have shot his lover in a fit of rage, then left the hotel?

On the surface, that felt plausible, though not exactly right. Taylor hadn't gotten the violent vibe from Florian; he seemed more like an earnest schoolteacher than a bully.

She shone the flashlight closer on the lock. There were scratches, like an impatient thief had jimmied it open. So much for that theory.

She took a deep breath and called his name quietly.

"Mr. Florian?"

Silence.

"Shine the light around, Taylor."

She did, and wasn't surprised to find the room empty.

13

0615 Hours

Florian has fainted, again. Before he succumbed to the pain, he was talking, but not saying the things I needed to hear. There are answers here, I know it. My father was not a traitor. My family did not have to die.

Many years of espionage has taught me well; eventually, everyone breaks. Watching Florian bleed and cry and lie isn't enough. I will speed up the process.

I go to the bathroom, gather a handful of water from the sink. The stream sputters and runs out as I watch. The room is cold; my hands are clumsy in the dark. Without the power, this is more difficult than I planned. The leads tied to Florian's chest and testicles will not work without electricity, and the fear of pain will not suffice. There has to be actual stimulus to coerce statements. Which means I'm back to the knife.

I splash the meager handful of water in his face, but it is enough. He sputters and his eyes open. I stand with my arms crossed, waiting for him to again register who I am, and why we are here.

"Angelie," he moans.

I drop to my knees, cajoling now, friendly.

"Talk to me, Thierry. Tell me what I need to know."

I wrap his wounds, binding them against the bleeding. It will feel better that way. He head lolls against me. I smell his fear. The infamous Thierry Florian, helpless and scared.

"That is all I have, Angelie. I know nothing else."

Kneeling back on my heels, I watch him. The letter tells me he is still lying.

"Thierry, they'll come for you soon. You must tell me the rest. Tell me, and this pain will stop." I tug on a lead attached between his legs, and he gulps a breath. His head bobs side to side, a metronome of hurt.

He whispers, "I would tell you you're wrong, but you will not believe me. "

"No, I won't believe anything less than the truth. You've been lying to me this entire time. For fifteen years, you've looked me in the face, knowing you killed my father. How could you? I thought you were my friend. I thought you were my father's friend."

He sighs, a great, dragging breath. "Dear Angelie, I am not lying. Your father panicked. We had a safe house prepared, guards to keep him safe, but someone got to him. Convinced him he was being double-crossed. Angelie, I do not know who this person was."

"Whoever it was, he told the truth. You double-crossed my father. You left him out in the cold to die." I toy with the knife at the edge of his groin. A lesser man would beg, plead, promise me anything, just to get the sharp edge away from their skin. Florian merely shakes his head.

"No, no, Angelie. I would never do that to him. He was my friend, yes, but I will be honest. He was too valuable. He was the greatest asset I'd ever trained. But the others, they had no compunction about lying to him to get what they wanted. And he chose to believe their faint words of promise, rather than follow my protocols. I wanted you all in the safe house in Annecy, he chose to buy the caravan and stay in the campgrounds. There was no way to protect him, he was too exposed. He exposed you all, and panicked when they came for him."

"More lies. This letter is dated three days before his death. He says he knew you were working for the Soviets. That you were a double agent. That's why he didn't trust you." I catch my tone, a petulant child. I add a sneer. "You dishonored your vows, Thierry, and their blood is on your hands."

14

0630 Hours

Taylor's theory about Florian being the shooter changed when she saw the blood by the window.

"Cherry, over here."

"Oh, no. This goes from bad to worse."

"It does, but don't lose hope just yet. There's not enough blood to assume the worst, not by a long shot. This is just a thimbleful, really." Taylor stared at the blood drops. They were drying around the edges, though the centers were still wet. Not fresh, but not old, either.

"The storm kicked into high gear at midnight. A time of death on Mr. Stamper would go a long way toward telling us whether Florian is still on site or was taken from the hotel."

Cherry shook her head. "You're not making me feel better. I have one man down, and one missing. Where the hell could he be?"

Taylor tucked her weapon back into its holster.

"I don't know. Anywhere—this campus is huge. But if he's still here, you're missing the bigger picture."

"The bigger picture?"

"It's entirely possible we're locked in this hotel with a cold-blooded murderer."

Cherry sat down hard on Florian's bed. "Oh, Lieutenant, trust me, I am well aware of this."

There was something in her tone, in the self-defeated flop on the bed.

Taylor squatted on the floor in front of the woman. "You sound like a woman who needs to get a load off her chest."

"I've screwed up. I didn't protect him. It's my fault."

"What do you mean, you've screwed up? Cherry, talk to me. What's really going on here?"

"You know who Thierry Florian is, I suspect?"

"He's worked with my fiancé, but I don't know him. I just met him tonight. He told me he's the head of the Macallan Group, and former clandestine services. The French, right, DGSE?"

"Always shy with his accomplishments, Thierry. That's what makes him such an excellent spy. His father was a leader in the French *Résistance* during World War II. When the French needed information about the Germans, François Florian would put himself in the worst possible situations, get arrested, then find ways to keep himself alive while he gathered information. When he had what he needed, he would escape and bring the information back to the resistance."

"An impressive man."

"Yes. Thierry was his youngest child, born well after the end of the war, but the tales his family told were intoxicating. While the rest of his siblings went into safe positions as doctors and lawyers, Thierry followed in his father's footsteps and joined what was then known as the DGSE—the Directorate-General for External Security."

"The French version of our CIA."

"Correct. He had an illustrious career. When he retired, he was the equivalent of our Director of Counterintelligence. But it was an especially covert side job that put him on his current path. Before he left he worked with the Alliance Base —do you know what that is?"

"An international cooperative of intelligence agencies, right? Working against Al Qaeda and other terrorist organizations?"

"Yes." She smiled, a little sadly. "Thierry has always ruffled feathers in the intelligence community with his theories. He feels cooperative intelligence is vital to deter more terrorist attacks on the Western world. But putting a bunch of spies together—well, friction was inevitable. He saw the ways the organization worked, and the ways it didn't. He was determined to perfect the mix. Hence, The Macallan Group."

"Why are you telling me this, Cherry? The man's CV isn't necessary for me to want to help."

"Bear with me a few moments more, Taylor. Thierry has made many enemies, and he is a target. It is entirely possible we have been infiltrated by someone he pissed off back in the day, and they're taking their chance at retribution."

"You handpicked the conference members, though, didn't you? Surely you wouldn't be so careless as to let a known combatant in."

She gave a little moan. "Spies, Taylor, we're all spies. Everyone working at cross-purposes. It's why I don't work with Thierry at Macallan. I have a clearer head than he when it comes to the simple fact that for centuries, we've been working against each other. It's all well and good to hope for cooperation, but ultimately, someone will want to get payback for some perceived grievance, and it all collapses."

"So who here had a vendetta against Thierry?"

"I don't know."

"Cherry, think. If you truly believe the killer is a part of the conference, think!"

Cherry went quiet, then, in a small voice, said, "There's one other person unaccounted for. Not from the conference, from our lives. I've known her for years. She is a friend, of sorts. Used to be a protégé of Thierry's before she went out on her own. We've worked in some pretty hairy places together. She went off grid a year ago, just when Thierry formed The Macallan Group. He wanted to recruit her, came looking, but I hadn't heard from her in several months. We put out some feelers, to see if anyone knew where she was. She was for hire, you see, a black market baby, very hush-hush."

Taylor knew what *for hire* meant. "She's an assassin."

Cherry leapt from the bed at the word, shaking her head. "I was silly to bring it up. There's no way she could be involved in this. She fights against evil. That's what drives her."

"I take it the feelers came up empty?"

"Yes. Nothing. She's gone gray."

"Gray?"

"Blending in. Hiding in plain sight. She's most likely setting up for a major job."

Taylor's voice rose. "A major job? Come on Cherry, talk to me. What kind of major job would this woman have to disappear for a year to prepare for?"

Cherry just shook her head. "I don't know. Before she left, she'd been . . . reckless. Taking on jobs that were out of character."

A sense of foreboding crept into Taylor's stomach. International assassins on the loose made her very uncomfortable—she'd come face to face with one herself a year earlier and hadn't enjoyed it a lick. A different tact was necessary; she could see Cherry was shutting down.

"Tell me this. Something about this set-up makes you think of this woman. What is it?"

Cherry pursed her lips. "Thierry alluded once, only once, that there was history between them. She still worked for DGSE then, was being groomed to move up the ladder. Something set her off and she went freelance, and I've never known what it was. But Thierry did. He must have. That's what he meant when he told me she'd become a black widow."

Ah. Interesting. "She'd get physically close to her prey, then kill them."

"Exactly. And she's one of the best at what she does. She's a legend, Taylor."

A legendary assassin. A wicked snowstorm. No power. One dead, one missing. This was just getting better and better.

"I take it the scene in Stamper's room looks familiar?"

"Very."

Taylor took the flashlight, went to the door, unlocked the bolt. Opened it into the dark hallway, then shined the light back into the room. There was no more time to lose.

"I need a name, Cherry."

The harsh light caught Cherry's face. She looked frightened and old, defeated, a pale specter in the darkness. She sat back down on the bed as if exhausted.

"She goes by many names, Taylor. But I believe her given name is Angelie Delacroix."

"That's a start. Let's go. We need to—"

Cherry shook her head, clearly the truth of the matter was finally sinking in. "No, Lieutenant, we have a bigger problem."

"Worse than one dead and one missing? Seriously?"

"Angelie's uncle is active MI-6. And he's downstairs."

15

I sit down on the floor near Florian. "Oncle Pierre told me the whole story last year. You were on the scene. You were the one who saved me, who took me to the hospital. But first you smashed me on the head so I wouldn't recognize you. Why did you kill my father, Thierry? My family? Why would you kill them and save me? *Pourquoi? Pourquoi?*"

I am shouting, losing control. I resist the urge to hit him again.

"Angelie. Angelie, it wasn't me. You have the story wrong."

I am beginning to believe Thierry Florian may be telling the truth. He is a proud man, one I've watched interrogate a hundred men. He is brave. And as he sits here bleeding, exposed, I must believe I know him well enough to recognize when he is telling the truth.

"Then what is the story, Thierry?"

"Don't make me tell you. Please."

This last word is spoken as softly as a lover's kiss. Finally, after hours of pain and fury, the great man is begging.

I tuck the muzzle of my Sig Sauer against his chin, and I raise his head so he is forced to meet my eyes.

"Tell me, and I will end your suffering."

He leans into the gun, his voice the harshest I've ever heard. "Kill me, and you will never get justice."

I stand and whirl away. Florian breathes out a sigh.

"You will not stop, will you? Ah, Angelie. I trained you well."

I run back to him, wrench his head back. Spit the words. "The truth, now. I am sick of playing this game."

"Pierre," he says, speaking out loud a terrible reality I've never fathomed. "It was Pierre. Your uncle killed your father."

Nausea overwhelms me. I drop my hand. "You're lying."

Florian shakes his head. He is disheveled, bloody, has absolutely nothing left to lose.

"I have never lied to you, Angelie. I have protected you, all along. I did not want you to suffer the pain of this knowledge. Indeed, I sheltered you from it since you were a child. Yes, it was I who rescued you. I got wind of your uncle's plan the day before the attack, though at the time I did not know he was behind it. I was in Germany. I drove all night to reach you, to take you all to safety.

"Your father ignored our attempts to get him into the safe house in Annecy. He was fleeing back to Paris on Pierre's orders. He believed Pierre was trying to help. He listened to him, and drove directly into the trap."

I stagger against the wall, tripping on something in the darkness. A pain I have not felt in twenty-five years rises in me, tears through my body, my brain, leaving me breathless.

"This cannot be the truth."

"It is the truth. I arrived on the scene moments after the shooting. Gregoire Campion was riding his bicycle down from the safe house, he met me on the westbound street. We were too late to save them, Angelie, too late by five minutes.

But you were still alive, clinging to your mother's skirts, covered in your parents' blood. I couldn't leave you there, and I could not let you see our faces. I did the only thing I could, which was rescue you and get you to a hospital. And I spent the next twenty years trying to determine what happened that day."

I try to digest this information.

"Why did you not tell me the moment you determined Pierre was behind the execution?"

"Ah. Angelie. And cause you that much more pain? Your uncle raised you, taught you well. He knew where your heart lay, knew you would try to avenge your parents some day. He is the reason you were hired into the DGSE. Gregoire Campion was worried about you from the first because he suspected Pierre's involvement, kept an eye on you, eased your path in the service. And you killed him. The man who watched over you, dead by your hand. Angelie, you disgrace yourself."

Campion, on the side of the angels?

I harden myself against Florian's words. "Pierre told me Campion was the one who let my parents' path slip, that he told the Iraqis where my father was going to be that day."

"That was Pierre, *mon cherie*. Pierre was receiving money, so much money, that he was willing to sacrifice his brother and his family. He has lied to you, Angelie, about many things. I am not a double agent. And I did not kill your father."

There is great finality to his words. I know he is telling the truth.

I slide down the wall, the pistol dangling between my legs.

Mon dieu. What have I done?

16

Taylor hustled down the four flights of stairs, Cherry on her heels. The minute they reached the bottom floor, Taylor asked, "What does he look like?"

"Mid-sixties, silver hair, six feet or so. He was wearing a blue suit last night, no tie, but I don't remember what he was wearing this morning. It was dark, and I was too concerned for Thierry and Ellis."

They burst into the lobby, raced to the room where everyone was staged. The room was still shrouded in darkness, and there was no more time to waste.

"Stay here. I'll find him."

"But you don't know what he looks like."

Taylor flashed the light on the ceiling a few times, creating a strobe effect that caught people's attention.

"Pierre Matthews. Are you in here?" she called.

Murmurs from the crowd, then one man stood, Taylor could see the outline of his bulk against the window.

"I'm here. Whatever is the matter?"

Taylor crossed the room, weaving between people, and took him by the arm. "Come with me, please, sir. There's a problem. We need your help."

The lobby was filled with natural light, the darkness finally easing in the early morning sun. The snow, she noticed, had stopped. Taylor turned off the flashlight, tucked it into her back pocket.

"What is this about?" Matthews asked.

"Sir, I'm Lieutenant Taylor Jackson, and you know Cherry Gregg. We have reason to believe you may be in danger. Would you please come with us?"

Matthews was nonplussed, but nodded. Taylor took the lead, Cherry flanked. They got him across into the bar, and Taylor got him into a corner where she felt he would be safest.

"You two have been scurrying in and out all night. What's happened? Where are Thierry and Ellis?"

Cherry spoke plainly. "Ellis is dead, and Thierry is missing."

"Bloody hell. Are you sure?"

"Do you know a woman named Angelie Delacroix?" Taylor asked.

Matthews sucked in a breath, and Taylor raised an eyebrow. "I'll take that as a yes."

She saw him debating with the answer. Finally, he replied, "She's my niece. Why are you asking about her? Is she all right?"

Cherry grabbed the man's forearm. "Pierre, she killed Ellis. She's taken Thierry."

Pierre froze. "Angelie is here? Are you sure?"

"Yes. She knows."

Taylor gave Cherry a sharp look. "She knows what?"

Cherry and Pierre were locked in a staring contest, no

words needed. Taylor recognized there was a bigger issue, something major they were keeping from her.

"Tell me right now what's happening, or I'm out. I'll go warm my hands by the fire and let Fred shoot me dirty looks."

Cherry nodded to Pierre. "You tell her."

"Ah, bugger me." He rubbed his hands over his face, the whiskers on his chin rasping loudly against his palm. "Angelie started acting up about two years ago. She didn't like the politics within the DGSE anymore, didn't want to play by the rules. We were all working together at the time, on the Allied project. The greater good. CIA, MI-6, DGSE, Freedom Forum, Futures Working Group—hell, even Pakistan's ISI was along for the ride. In the middle of the fuck-up in Benghazi, she got a bug up her bum about some old case, took off for parts unknown. All we've heard from her since has been at the end of a gun—she's left a trail of bodies all over Europe, the last one found just two days ago in London."

"Gone rogue?" Taylor couldn't help the skepticism that slipped into her tone.

"That's right. You must understand, Lieutenant, Angelie is marked by tragedy. Her parents were killed in an ambush outside Annecy, France, twenty-five years ago. She was the only survivor, and she spent her whole life searching for the killers."

Taylor heard the past tense. "*Spent* her whole life? She's found her parents' murderers?"

He cut his eyes at Cherry, who nodded imperceptibly. "She found him at last. Gregoire Campion, her latest victim, the body from two days ago. She found a letter with the details. He sold out her parents, my own brother, and for what? Money? Security? Who can know the true heart of a man like that, Lieutenant? I am sure his death assuaged many of Angelie's troubles."

Taylor processed that for a moment. "If she found the

man who did it, then why would she come here and kill Ellis Stamper? Why kidnap Thierry Florian?"

"Stamper was most likely collateral damage. Florian worked with Campion back then. He was the DGSE equivalent of a station chief in Geneva, Switzerland, just north of Annecy. She must think he was a part of the plot."

"Was he?" Taylor asked, trying to reconcile this information against her brief meeting with Florian and Cherry's praise-filled backgrounder. He didn't seem capable of that level of treachery. Taylor prided herself on being able to read people; she hadn't caught a whiff of evil from Florian.

"I don't know. He denied it, said he was there trying to protect them, but I never got the whole story. My brother's death was a terrible time for us all. I took Angelie in, raised her as my own daughter. She had a massive memory block on what happened that day—after the head injury, it was all gone. She took a hard blow, probably pistol-whipped. It was a miracle that she survived. Florian had his eye on her from the very beginning. You know what they say: keep your friends close, but keep your enemies closer."

Taylor didn't like Pierre Matthews. He was slick; the answers were too pat, too prepared, and something in her gut told her he was lying. Granted, a situation like this, about family, so personal, there was no reason to tell her the whole truth. Yes, he was lying. She'd bet her life on it. About what, she didn't know, and that made him very dangerous to her in this situation. And she realized Cherry knew more than she was letting on, too.

"Are you armed, Pierre?"

"My weapon is in my room. Why?"

Thank God for small favors.

"Well, your friend, or your enemy, is missing, and Cherry believes it's likely your niece is prowling around this hotel with her own loaded weapon. We need to figure out where

Thierry Florian is, and take your niece into custody while we assess what happened last night."

Cherry came back to life, finally. "Without lights for those dark hallways, or the ability to open multiple doors without tearing this place apart, how do we search?"

Taylor shrugged. "We need to find a way to get the lights turned on."

17

I unbind Florian's ties, my fingers working quickly. It would have been so easy to simply kick his chair, let him fall into the pool. He would have been gone, his storied life a sudden footnote, the weight of the chair keeping him under.

There will be no more deaths, save one.

Florian stands cautiously, rubbing his wrists.

"Clothes?"

I gesture to the right, by the hot tub, where his clothes are folded in a neat pile. He says nothing, simply turns his back on me and dresses. I walk slowly, carefully, around the edges of the pool. It would be so easy to fling myself into the dark water. It is salt water; I can smell the brine. Like floating in an ocean, sinking deep beneath the waves. My parents used to take us to the sea, to Le Lavendou, and we'd stay at the Beau Rivage and prune ourselves in the azure water from sunup to sundown.

I did not know these holidays were paid for by secrets. Blueprints and plans for rapidly-developed forms of kinetic energy, stolen by my father from his employer, and sold to the Iraqis. Or the Russians. Syrians and Pakistanis. Whoever was paying at that particular moment.

My father was a mole. An asset. Turned for the DGSE's use, a puppet on a string, only useful while he could help in the race to nuclear proliferation supremacy.

And me? I became the very person my father hated. The nameless, faceless people he put his trust in, the mechanics of his dead drops and microfiche holders and tradecraft.

I could not help it. *Mon oncle*, he showed me how valuable this work was. How I could change the world, one turned asset at a time.

If my father lived, would that have changed? Would I have been so heavily recruited? So well-trained? Honed into a weapon of immeasurable worth?

I think not.

Florian is watching me. "Angelie. You must leave."

My toe yanks back from the water. I stare into Florian's eyes, unable to see clearly for the lack of light.

"Go. I will handle this situation. Get away from this place."

"Why would you have me save myself, Thierry Florian? Why should I not turn myself in? Suffer the consequences of my actions? I have killed this night. Taken your friend from you. You should want my head."

He smiles, the tiniest lift of the corners of his mouth. And I know what he will say next.

"What a curious turn of phrase. *Oui, cherie*, I very much want your head. And I shall have it. You work for me now, Angelie. Again. Again and forever. Now, go."

I am defeated. For a moment I think to kill him anyway. Then I can be free. But I listen.

I stash the gun in my waistband, gather my tools, and without a word, head for the door. There is a storm. I know this; I see the piles of snow against the door. How I will get away isn't clear. I had no plans for escape. This was intended to be my last hurrah. A suicide mission. But now that I know the truth? As they say, the show must go on.

The hallways are still dark and quiet. The blueprint of the hotel plays through my head. I need to turn left at the gym, it will lead me to the basement, which has an exit onto a back expanse of land. There is a shelter one hundred yards from the hotel, a place I can regroup until I can reach my exit.

A voice from the other side of the pool. "Hey. Hey, stop!"

My weapon is pointed at the voice before I can form a coherent thought.

18

0700 Hours

A fuel truck, riding slowly behind a snowplow, arrived at seven in the morning to everyone's cheers. The fuel was pumped into the basement generators, the lights flickered to life, and a semblance of normality restored. People scattered back to their rooms to get some sleep and check in with loved ones.

Taylor was glad of it; now they could do a proper search, and run a crime scene unit through Stamper and Florian's rooms.

Cherry and Pierre had been huddled together in a corner of the bar for the past fifteen minutes, backs to the wall, eyes darting to the entrance every few moments, and Taylor wondered what sort of story they were concocting. Self-preservation, preparation, a cover-up, she didn't know, only that they were both acting like Angelie Delacroix was going to burst through the wall yelling *yippie ki-yay* and shoot up the place.

Taylor left them alone, paced the bar. Florian's disappearance was gnawing at her. She wanted to strike off and look for him, but knew how foolish that was, especially if the über-assassin was still on site. They needed manpower, backup, K9 units, the works. Sure enough, fifteen minutes later, the Calvert County Sheriff, a decent-looking man named Evans, arrived, summoned by the report of a murder.

Taylor and Cherry explained the situation. To his credit, he took down their stories with a raised eyebrow and only a few head shakes. He went upstairs, came down with a grim expression, asked Taylor several probing questions, then said, "Lieutenant, glad you were here. Situation might have gotten further out of control. There are more people coming, State Police, FBI, K9. Storm's holding everyone up. We're going to need you to give your official statement, so get comfy."

"Can't I help? I don't want to sit around doing nothing."

"It's going to take more than two of us to search this place." He smiled, kindly enough. "You've done your part. Why don't you head to your room and get some rest? I'd lock my door, though my guess is Florian and this Delacroix woman are long gone. Timing wise, the streets were still passable until after midnight. The hotel lobby's videotape wasn't recording, so that's useless. Just need to bring in the troops and get this place searched and processed. You know how it goes."

Taylor did, and knew her role in the situation was finished. With the jurisdictional cops on scene, she was relegated back to conference attendee and witness. Which was weird.

But Evans had a point. A little sleep wouldn't go amiss.

She interrupted another confab between Pierre and Cherry.

"Cherry, I'm going to go up to my room. Call me if they find Florian, okay?"

19

Taylor had to detour to her room—though the power was back on, the elevators were still off-limits. She pulled a site map off the concierge desk and glanced at it. The back staircase would be closer to her room. She took the hallway toward the gym, the scent leading her toward the pool and the hot tub. Ah, a hot bath in that giant tub upstairs would be lovely, though she doubted the water heaters were going to get suitable power from the generators to pump water hot enough for her taste.

She pushed through the pool doors and immediately knew something was wrong. Instinct, coupled with the chair at the edge of the pool, ropes coiled neatly by its legs. She drew her weapon and went into a defensive stance. The glass windows in the place were wavy, giving weak light that shimmered against the pool water. She went slowly, searching, until she saw the open door to the lifeguard office. And inside was Thierry Florian, eyes closed, leaning back on a longue chair. Blood soaked his shirt, and he was pale as a ghost. Asleep, or dead?

She rushed to him, put her fingers against his carotid. A steady beat, and her breath whooshed out. He started, eyes opening. "Angelie, I told you—"

He cut himself off when he saw Taylor.

"Where is she?"

"I don't know what you're talking about."

"Mr. Florian, please. Ellis Stamper is dead. You've obviously been tortured. I know all about Angelie Delacroix. Cherry and Pierre Matthews filled me in. Where is she?"

He licked his lips, which were cracked and bloody. "Gone," he whispered.

She helped him sit up.

"Why aren't you dead? It looks like she gave you quite a working over."

He smiled, though the action obviously caused him pain. "You are blunt, aren't you, Lieutenant? Angelie didn't want me dead. She just wanted information."

"Somehow, I don't believe that is the whole story. The Sheriff is here, and there's about to be a whole wad of law enforcement on his tail. Is she still here, Thierry? Tell me the truth."

"She left ten minutes ago. You won't catch her."

Taylor met his eyes. "Watch me."

20

0735 Hours

Taylor called Cherry, told her to share what was happening with the Sheriff, and to send backup immediately. She shoved her cell phone in her pocket and press checked her Glock. It was habit, a cop's unconscious movement.

Florian tried to stop her. "You're wasting your time."

He tried to rise, but the blood loss had taken its toll.

"You stay here and guard the pool. When the Sheriff's people come, show them the way."

"On your head be it," Florian said. "Don't say I didn't warn you."

Taylor gave him a smile and started off.

One thing Taylor had gathered about Angelie Delacroix, there would be signs of her passage. Morbid signs. Since Taylor hadn't seen any on her way in, she exited opposite the door she'd originally come through, toward the north end of the pool, right out into the hallway that led to the back entrance of the hotel. The light was startling here, she had to blink to adjust.

She took in the whiteness outside, knew there was no way anyone could get out of there without leaving a mess.

It didn't take long to find the trail. Footprints led toward a small outbuilding about fifty yards away. Backup was moments behind, so Taylor stepped out into the freezing cold.

Her hands went numb almost immediately, but she kept the weapon up and ready. The going was slow, the snow drifting to her waist in places. The chill wind was rising again, Taylor recognized the feeling. This was a temporary reprieve; there was more snow on the way.

Her feet were snug in her boots, but snow was sliding down the calf and into the leather. A fine shiver started, and with it, her common sense.

You're an idiot, Taylor. Go back inside and let the locals freeze their asses off.

She could hear them now, closing in. She started edging backwards. As she turned, there was a woman, standing in her path.

Taylor froze. The woman was small—Taylor had a good six inches on her—but her weapon was pointed right at Taylor's head.

"And who might you be?" the woman asked, her accent clearly French.

"Police. Put the gun down, Angelie. You can't rack up any more bodies today, you're already going away for a very long time."

The woman cocked her head to the side. The gun didn't waver.

"I think you are the one who needs to disarm yourself, Lieutenant Jackson. Yes, I know your name. It's next to that smiling photograph on the program in Thierry's room. A profiler, are you?"

"Homicide. You're under arrest. Put the damn gun down, now."

"I think not," Angelie said, then before Taylor could blink, she took off, through the snow, toward a stone wall that barely peeked out under its white blanket.

"Shit!"

Taylor took off after her, amazed at Angelie's prowess in the snow. Taylor was too tall, too ungainly, to make quick progress. There was only one thing to do.

Taylor stopped and fired, and the bullet found its target. Angelie spun to the side, and Taylor heard her cry out.

"Drop the weapon, Angelie, and I won't do that again."

Shouts rang out from the building to her left, the Sheriff's deputies were coming. Angelie heard them as well, didn't hesitate. She fired off several rounds, spraying them wildly behind her, forcing Taylor face down in the snow.

Taylor rolled to her right, flipped over and up onto her knees and aimed again.

Angelie's left arm was dragging by her side, but she kept running, a dead sprint through the heavy snow. She reached the stone wall before Taylor could get off a second round, and disappeared behind it.

It took Taylor a full minute to scramble to her feet and reach the spot.

"She's here," she called to the deputies, who were wading through the snow well behind her.

Carefully, slowly, weapon first, Taylor looked over the edge of the wall. Beyond it was a steep slope. It was terraced, a vineyard in the summertime, staggered levels that ran down the hill, demarcated by stone barriers. One section dropped off into the beach below. Taylor figured it must be a forty-foot drop.

Angelie Delacroix was crouched against the stone barrier above the beach, back to the ocean, watching Taylor. She was trapped, and bleeding. Their eyes met.

Taylor edged closer. *Take the shot, Taylor, take the shot. You can end this, right here.*

She took a breath to steady her hands, shaking in the cold. Her finger rested on the trigger. Just a fraction of movement, and the bullet would take Angelie Delacroix in the forehead.

And in that moment, Angelie raised her weapon toward Taylor in a sort of salute and smiled, crooked, knowing, then jumped off the ledge, toward the sea.

Taylor gritted her teeth and scrambled over the wall. *Damn it. Damn it all.* She'd had a clear shot. She shouldn't have hesitated. But she recognized something in the woman's eyes. Something dark, and unimaginable to those who hadn't been faced with taking a life. And Taylor had chosen that route, too many times.

The first bullet had hit Angelie in the shoulder. Taylor had shot to maim, not kill. She made a choice, right or wrong, and now her prey was gone.

She pointed the weapon at the barrier, just where the woman had disappeared. Listened, but heard nothing.

"Police!" she shouted. "Show me your hands."

Silence. The waves crashed below, a seagull cried. Silence amplified by the dizzying expanse of white before her, her voice echoed slightly. To her right, disturbed by the deputies making their way closer, a bird took wing, startled by the noise, sent her heart right to her throat.

Taylor ducked her head, took a deep breath in through her nose, and leading with her Glock, looked over the edge. She was prepared for what she found.

Nothing.

There was no sign of Angelie Delacroix.

All that was left of her was a spattering of blood drops on the snow, like a shower of rubies dashed onto white velvet.

When Taylor had hesitated, that split second when she decided she couldn't kill, not again, something like realization had dawned in Angelie's eyes. She had recognized that Taylor would not fire again.

That knowing smile would haunt Taylor's dreams.

A choice. Right or wrong, Taylor had let her get away.

She slumped against the stone. The deputies finally reached her, Sheriff Evans at their head.

"Where is she, where is she?"

"She jumped."

Evans looked slightly relieved, holstered his weapon.

"Then she's dead. That's a fifty-foot fall. We'll find her body on the beach."

"I don't think so," she said, and he looked at her queerly.

"Of course we will. What the hell were you doing, out here chasing her down alone? I thought I told you to stand down."

Taylor turned to face him, the wind whipping her hair around her face.

"I was doing my job."

And the sun broke through the clouds.

EPILOGUE

January 15, 2014
London, England
0300 Hours

I stand over his bed. He sleeps with one arm tossed over his head. I recognize the position; my father, his brother, also slept in this way—careless, with abandon.

He is quiet. No snoring, just deep, rhythmic breaths.

I want him to see. I want him to know. I rub my shoulder, warding off the pain from the ghost of a bullet that lodged against my scapula, courtesy of the blonde ice queen. I'll never forget, and she knew that would be the case. But I will leave her alone. I have learned a hard truth in the past few months.

Not all scores are meant to be settled.

But some . . . some beg for closure.

I slide his covers down with the end of my weapon, and lean close, so I can whisper in his ear.

"Oncle Pierre. Time to wake up."

ABOUT THE STORY

WHITEOUT is one of a triad of stories that first appeared in STORM SEASON, a collection of novellas with my dear friends Erica Spindler and Alex Kava. To see how this monstrous storm affects two other precincts dealing with diabolical killers, purchase the full book, STORM SEASON.

AUTHOR'S NOTE

I've always looked at short stories as a way to have a bit of fun with my writing. In my day job, I write psychological thrillers. I'd written three novels before I ever tried my hand at short fiction. But when I did, I discovered an entirely new world.

I spent a great deal of time telling my peers I couldn't write short stories. They kept pushing me, and pushing me, until I finally gave it a shot.

That story was "Prodigal Me." I submitted it to *Writer's Digest* and promptly forgot about it. You can imagine my surprise when I received an email from Chuck Sambuchino saying I'd won an honorable mention in their annual short fiction contest.

Perhaps I could write shorts after all.

Soon after, I attended my first writer's conference, where I met a fabulous writer named Duane Swierczynski. I asked Duane about some short fiction markets, and he suggested I send a story to his friend Bryon Quertermous, who ran an e-zine called *Demolition*. I quickly wrote another story and submitted it. Bryon loved everything but the title, which we agreed to change to "X." It was my first published piece.

My love of the short form grew from there. I began placing stories, writing for anthologies, the works. I grew to love the freedom and limitations of the form, and I still use it as a playground of sorts, a way to stretch my wings and explore genres I wouldn't normally write in.

My short stories are little slices, vignettes. Crimes of the heart, the mind and the soul. The bits and pieces that fell from my mind while I was writing long-form novels, the ideas that didn't have a place in my current work. Some are quite short, others bloomed into novellas.

With the advent of independent publishing, I decided to start my own house, Two Tales Press, in order to share these sweet little lies with you. I do hope you'll enjoy them.

—J.T. Ellison
Nashville, 2015

photo credit: Krista Lee Photography

New York Times bestselling author J.T. Ellison writes dark psychological thrillers starring Nashville Homicide **Lt. Taylor Jackson** and medical examiner **Dr. Samantha Owens,** and penned the Nicholas Drummond series with #1 *New York Times* bestselling author Catherine Coulter. Cohost of the EMMY Award-winning television show, *A Word on Words*, Ellison lives in Nashville with her husband and twin kittens.

Join her email list, or follow her on **Facebook, Twitter,** and **Instagram.**

SNEAK PEEKS

(YOU LUCKY READER!)

For your enjoyment, I've included three excerpts for you. The first is a peek at my standalone thriller, **LIE TO ME**. The next is from my newest Taylor Jackson novel, **FIELD OF GRAVES**, which is actually a prequel to the series. Last but not least is an excerpt from one of my favorite writers, Laura Benedict, who is writing a brilliant Southern Gothic series called Bliss House. The excerpt is from her latest novel, **THE ABAN-DONED HEART**, available now. I hope you love them all!

LIE TO ME

EXCERPT

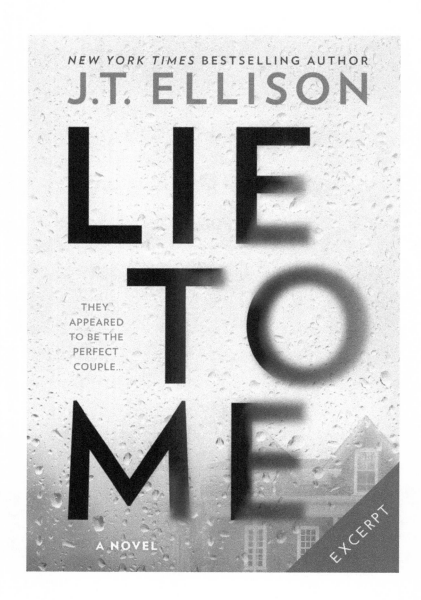

NEW YORK TIMES BESTSELLING AUTHOR

J.T. ELLISON

LIE
TO
ME

THEY
APPEARED
TO BE THE
PERFECT
COUPLE...

A NOVEL

EXCERPT

MIRA Books
a division of Harlequin
225 Duncan Mill Road
Toronto, Ontario M3B 3K9
Canada

PROLOGUE

You aren't going to like me very much. Oh, maybe in your weaker moments, you'll feel sorry for me, and use those feelings of warmth and compassion and insightful understanding to excuse my actions. You'll say to yourself, "Poor little girl. She couldn't help herself." Or, "Can you blame her? After all she's been through?" Perhaps you'll even think, "She was born to this. It is not her fault."

Of course it's my fault. I chose this path. Yes, I feel as if I have no choice, that I'm driven to do it, that there are voices in my head that push me to the dark side.

But I also know right from wrong. I know good from evil. I may be compelled to ruin the lives in front of me, but I could walk away if I wanted.

Couldn't I?

Never mind that. Back to you.

Truly, deep down, you are going to despise me. I am the rot that lives in the floorboards of your house. I am the spider that scuttles away when you shine light in my corner, ever watching, ever waiting. I am the shard of glass that slits the skin of your bare foot. I am all the bad things that happen to you.

I steal things.

I kill things.

I leave a trail of destruction in my wake that is a sight to behold, wave after wave of hate that will overwhelm you until you sink to the bottom of my miserable little ocean, and once you've drowned I will feed on your flesh and turn your bones to dust.

You're mine now. You are powerless against me. So don't bother fighting it.

I hope you enjoy the show.

ETHAN

"Chaos is a name for any order that produces confusion in our minds."

— GEORGE SANTAYANA

WE FIND A BODY

The body was in the woods off a meandering state road that led into a busy, charming historical downtown. It was completely obscured from view, deeply hidden, under several pine boughs and a thick layer of nature's detritus. Synthetic clothing was melted to the flesh, making it difficult to tell the body's race or gender at a glance. Closer investigation showed hair that was long and a curious shade: not blonde, not red, possibly chemically-treated. The left hand held evidence of rings, possibly a wedding set, and so the body was eventually determined as female.

The shroud of melt and bough had not stopped the forever daisy-chain progression of decay. Instar maggots and adult flies delighted in their found treat. A genus party started soon after. Diptera and Coleoptera were evident three days in, paving the way for the coming colonization of Calliphoridae. Though the body was burned beyond ready recognition, the insects didn't seem to mind; it was simply a barbecue feast to them.

Outside of this natural progression, the body lay undisturbed for two days. Birds of prey flew in long, lazy circles overhead. Cars drove past less than fifty yards away, drivers unknowing, uncaring, that one of their own lay rotting nearby.

Three Days Gone, a stray but severe thunderstorm knocked free several of the funereal branches, allowing the body to be exposed, pelted by hail breaking through the leafy canopy. The heavy rains wet the ground and allowed the body to sink deeper into the muck, where it canted on its side.

Four Days Gone, the body was ravaged by a starving coyote, forty-two razor teeth shredding everything available.

Five Days Gone, the body disarticulated, the fire and the heat and the wet and the insects and the coyote and the natural progression of things breaking it down quickly and without thought to the effects this would have on the loved ones. The idea of a non-intact body was sometimes more than people could take.

Six Days Gone, they found her.

SOMETHING'S MISSING

Franklin, Tennessee
Now

Ethan found the note ten minutes after he rolled out of bed that Tuesday, the Tuesday that would change everything. He came downstairs yawning, scratching his chest, to... nothing. Empty space, devoid of wife.

Sutton always began her morning at the table with a bowl of cereal, a piece of fruit, and a cup of tea and read the paper, scoffing at the innumerable typos—the paper was going under, paying for decent copyediting was the least of their worries. A bowl full of cereal, a glass of milk and a spoon would be laid out for him, the sports page folded neatly by his seat. Always. Always.

But this morning, there was no evidence Sutton had been in the kitchen. No newspaper, no bowl. No wife.

He called for her. There was no answer. He searched through the house. Her bag was in her office, her cellphone, her laptop. Her license was stashed in her small wallet, all her credit cards present and accounted for, a twenty folded in half shoved behind them.

She must have gone for a run.

He felt a spark of pleasure at the thought. Sutton, once, had been a health nut. She'd run or walked or done yoga every day, something physical, something to keep her body moving and in shape. And what a shape—the woman was a knockout, willowy and lithe, strong legs and delicate ankles, tendons tight and gleaming like a thoroughbred. A body she sculpted to match his own, to fit with him.

Ethan Montclair couldn't have a dog for a wife, no. He needed someone he could trot out at cocktail parties who looked smashing in a little black dress. And not only looked good, but sounded good. He needed a partner on all levels—physical and intellectual. Maybe it was shallow of him, but he was a good looking man, drew a lot of attention, and not only did he want his wife to be stunning, he wanted her to be smart, too. And Sutton fit the bill.

He knew they made a powerful, attractive couple. Looks and brains and success, so much success. That was their thing.

After Dashiell, she'd bounced back into shape like the champion racehorse she was, though later, when their world collapsed, she'd become tired and bloated and swollen with medications and depression, and she no longer took any interest in being beautiful and fit.

That she'd decided to start running again gave him hope. So much hope.

Spirits lifted, he went back to the sunny, happy kitchen and got his own bowl, his own milk. Made a pot of tea, whistling. Went for the stevia—no sugar for the health-conscious Montclairs, no, never.

That was when he saw it. Small. White. Lined. Torn from

a spiral bound notebook, a Clairefontaine, Sutton's favorite for the smooth, lovely paper.

This... thing... was incongruous with the rest of their spotless kitchen. Sutton was above all things a pathological neatnik. She'd never just leave something lying about.

All the happiness fled. He knew. He just knew. He'd been all wrong. She hadn't gone running.

He picked up the note.

Dear Ethan,

I'm sorry to do this to you, but I need some time away. I've been unhappy, you know that. This shouldn't come as a big surprise. Forgive me for being a coward. Forgive me, for so many things.

Don't look for me.

S

SHE WAS GONE.

He felt something squeezing in his chest, a pain of sorts, and realized that his heart had just broken. He'd always thought that a stupid, silly term, but now he knew. It could happen, it was happening. He was being torn in two, torn to shreds. No wonder there were rites warning against this —*What therefore God hath joined together, let not man put asunder.*

God was ripping him apart in punishment, and he deserved it. He deserved it all.

He didn't cry. There were no tears left for either of them to shed.

He put the note down carefully, as if it were a bomb that might go off with the wrong touch. Went to their bedroom. Nothing seemed out of place. Her brush, her makeup case, her toothbrush, all lined up carefully on the marble. Her suitcase was in the closet.

He went back downstairs to her office, at the back of the house. Doubled checked.

Her laptop was on her desk.

Her cellphone was in the charger.

Her purse was on the floor next to her chair.

Her wallet inside, the smiling DMV photo that made her look like a model.

Like a zombie, he moved back to the kitchen. He opened the refrigerator and got out the milk. Poured cereal in the bowl. Dropped the stevia into his tea. Sat at the empty table, stared at the spot where his wife's head should have been.

What was he supposed to do now? Where could she be? He ran through the possibilities, the places she loved, discarding one after another. Surely he was wrong in his thinking. Surely she'd simply run away, to one of her friends. That's where she'd gone. Should he call Ivy and see if Sutton was camped in her kitchen, instead of his? Should he give her some time, and space, like she asked?

She left without her things, Ethan. Sutton's lifelines are her laptop and phone. It's her office, her world.

A dawning realization. Sutton hadn't shaken the depression, not completely. She was still prone to fits of melancholy. She might have done something stupid, crazy. She'd tried once before, after... Oh, God. Her words. Perhaps she was telling him exactly what she'd done.

I'm a coward. Forgive me. Don't look for me.

He threw the bowl of cereal across the room.

"Bloody fucking hell. You selfish, heartless bitch."

ENJOY THIS PEEK INTO LIE TO ME?

ORDER YOURS!

FIELD OF GRAVES

EXCLUSIVE EXCERPT

J.T.

NEW YORK TIMES BESTSELLING AUTHOR

ELLISON

FIELD
OF
GRAVES

"ELLISON CLEARLY BELONGS IN THE TOP ECHELON OF THRILLER WRITERS."
—*Booklist*, starred review, on *What Lies Behind*

MIRA Books
a division of Harlequin
225 Duncan Mill Road
Toronto, Ontario M3B 3K9
Canada

PROLOGUE

Taylor picked up her portable phone for the tenth time in ten minutes. She hit Redial, heard the call connect and start ringing, then clicked the Off button and returned the phone to her lap. Once she made this call, there was no going back. Being right wouldn't make her the golden girl. If she were wrong—well, she didn't want to think about what could happen. Losing her job would be the least of her worries.

Damned if she did. Damned if she didn't.

She set the phone on the pool table and went down the stairs of her small two-story cabin. In the kitchen, she opened the door to the refrigerator and pulled out a Diet Coke. She laughed to herself. As if more caffeine would give her the courage to make the call. She should try a shot of whiskey. That always worked in the movies.

She snapped open the tab and stood staring out of her kitchen window. It had been dark for hours—the moon gone and the inky blackness outside her window impenetrable—but in an hour the skies would lighten. She would have to make a decision by then.

She turned away from the window and heard a loud crack. The lights went out. She jumped a mile, then giggled nervously, a hand to her chest to stop the sudden pounding.

Silly girl, she thought. *The lights go out all the time. There was a Nashville Electric Service crew on the corner when you drove in earlier; they must have messed up the line and a power surge caused the lights to blow. It happens every time NES works on the lines. Now stop it. You're a grown woman. You're not afraid of the dark.*

She reached into her junk drawer and groped for a flashlight. Thumbing the switch, she cursed softly when the light didn't shine. Batteries, where were the batteries?

She froze when she heard the noise and immediately went on alert, all of her senses going into overdrive. She strained her ears, trying to hear it again. Yes, there it was. A soft scrape off the back porch. She took a deep breath and sidled out of the kitchen, keeping close to the wall, moving lightly toward the back door. She brought her hand to her side and found nothing. Damn it. She'd left her gun upstairs.

The tinkling of breaking glass brought her up short.

The French doors leading into the backyard had been breached. It was too late to head upstairs and get the gun. She would have to walk right through the living room to get to the stairs. Whoever had just broken through her back door was not going to let her stroll on by. She started edging back toward the kitchen, holding her breath, as if that would help her not make any noise.

She didn't see the fist, only felt it crack against her jaw. Her eyes swelled with tears, and before she could react, the fist connected again. She spun and hit the wall face-first. The impact knocked her breath out. Her lips cut on the edge of her teeth; she tasted blood. The intruder grabbed her as she started to slide down the wall. Yanked her to her feet and put his hands around her throat, squeezing hard.

Now she knew exactly where her attacker was, and she fought back with everything she had. She struggled against him, quickly realizing she was in trouble. He was stronger than her, bigger than her. And he was there to kill.

She went limp, lolled bonelessly against him, surprising him with the sudden weight. He released one arm in response, and she took that moment to whirl around and shove with all her might. It created some space between them, enabling her to slip out of his grasp. She turned quickly but crashed into the slate end table. He was all over her. They struggled their way into the living room. She began to plan. Kicked away again.

Her attacker lunged after her. She used the sturdy side table to brace herself and whipped out her left arm in a perfect jab, aiming lower than where she suspected his chin would be. She connected perfectly and heard him grunt in pain. Spitting blood out of her mouth in satisfaction, she followed the punch with a kick to his stomach, heard the *whoosh* of his breath as it left his body. He fell hard against the wall. She spun away and leapt to the stairs. He jumped up to pursue her, but she was quicker. She pounded up the stairs as fast as she could, rounding the corner into the hall just as her attacker reached the landing. Her weapon was in its holster, on the bookshelf next to the pool table, right where she had left it when she'd gone downstairs for the soda. She was getting careless. She should never have taken it off her hip. With everything that was happening, she shouldn't have taken for granted that she was safe in her own home.

Her hand closed around the handle of the weapon. She pulled the Glock from its holster, whipped around to face the door as the man came tearing through it. She didn't stop to think about the repercussions, simply reacted. Her hand rose by instinct, and she put a bullet right between his eyes. His momentum carried him forward a few paces. He was only five feet from her, eyes black in death, when he dropped with a thud.

She heard her own ragged breathing. She tasted blood and raised a bruised hand to her jaw, feeling her lips and her teeth gingerly. Son of a bitch had caught her right in the jaw and loosened two molars. The adrenaline rush left her. She collapsed on the floor next to the lifeless body. She might have even slept for a moment.

The throbbing in her jaw brought her back. Morning was beginning to break, enough to see the horrible mess in front of her. The cat was sitting on the pool table, watching her curiously.

Rising, she took in the scene. The man was collapsed on her game room floor, slowly leaking blood on her Berber carpet. She peered at the stain.

That's going to be a bitch to get out.

She shook her head to clear the cobwebs. What an inane thing to say. Shock, she must be going into shock. How long had they fought? Had it been only five minutes? Half an hour? She felt as though she had struggled against him for days; her body was tired and sore. Never mind the blood caked around her mouth. She put her hand up to her face. Make that her nose too.

She eyed the man again. He was facedown and angled slightly to one side. She slipped her toes under his right arm and flipped him over with her foot. The shot was true; she could see a clean entry wound in his forehead. Reaching down out of habit, she felt for his carotid pulse, but there was nothing. He was definitely dead.

"Oh, David," she said. "You absolute idiot. Look what you've made me do."

Now the shit was absolutely going to hit the fan. It was time to make the call.

CHAPTER 1

Three months later
Nashville, Tennessee

Bodies, everywhere bodies, a field of graves, limbs and torsos and heads, all left above ground. The feeling of dirt in her mouth, grimy and thick; the whispers from the dead, long arms reaching for her as she passed through the carnage. Ghostly voices, soft and sibilant. "Help us. Why won't you help us?"

Taylor jerked awake, sweating, eyes wild and blind in the darkness. The sheets twisted around her body in a claustrophobic shroud, and she struggled to get them untangled. She squeezed her eyes shut, willed her breathing back to normal, trying to relax, to let the grisly images go. When she opened her eyes, the room was still dark but no longer menacing. Her screams had faded away into the silence. The cat jumped off the bed with a disgruntled meow in response to her thrashing.

She laid her head back on the pillow, swallowed hard, still unable to get a full breath.

Every damn night. She was starting to wonder if she'd ever sleep well again.

She wiped a hand across her face and looked at the clock: 6:10 A.M. The alarm was set for seven, but she wasn't going to get any more rest. She might as well get up and get ready for work. Go in a little early, see what horrors had captured the city overnight.

She rolled off the bed, trying hard to forget the dream. Showered, dressed, dragged on jeans and a black cashmere T-shirt under a black motorcycle jacket, stepped into her favorite boots. Put her creds in her pocket and her gun on her hip. Pulled her wet hair off her face and into a ponytail.

Time to face another day.

She was in her car when the call came. "Morning, Fitz. What's up?"

"Morning, LT. We have us a body at the Parthenon."

"I'll be right there."

IT MIGHT HAVE BECOME a perfect late-autumn morning. The sky was busy, turning from white to blue as dawn rudely forced its way into day. Birds were returning from their mysterious nocturnal errands, greeting and chattering about the night's affairs. The air was clear and heavy, still muggy from the overnight heat but holding a hint of coolness, like an ice cube dropped into a steaming mug of coffee. The sky would soon shift to sapphire the way only autumn skies do, as clear and heavy as the precious stone itself.

The beauty of the morning was lost on Lieutenant Taylor Jackson, Criminal Investigation Division, Nashville Metro Police. She snapped her long body under the yellow crime scene tape and looked around for a moment. Sensed the looks from the officers around her. Straightened her shoulders and marched toward them.

Metro officers had been traipsing around the crime scene control area like it was a cocktail party, drinking coffee and chatting each other up as though they'd been apart for weeks, not hours. The grass was already littered with cups, cigarette butts, crumpled notebook paper, and at least one copy of the morning's sports section from *The Tennessean*. Taylor cursed silently; they knew better than this. One of these yahoos was going to inadvertently contaminate a crime scene one of these days, sending her team off on a wild-goose chase. Guess whose ass would be in the proverbial sling then?

She stooped to grab the sports page, surreptitiously glanced at the headline regaling the Tennessee Titans' latest win, then crumpled it into a firm ball in her hands.

Taylor didn't know what information about the murder had leaked out over the air, but the curiosity factor had obviously kicked into high gear. An officer she recognized from another sector was cruising by to check things out, not wanting to miss out on all the fun. Media vans lined the street. Joggers pretending not to notice anything was happening nearly tripped trying to see what all the fuss was about. Exactly what she needed on no sleep: everyone willing to help, to get in and screw up her crime scene.

Striding toward the melee, she tried to tell herself that it wasn't their fault she'd been up all night. At least she'd had a shower and downed two Diet Cokes, or she would have arrested them all.

She reached the command post and pasted on a smile. "Mornin', kids. How many of you have dragged this crap through my crime scene?" She tossed the balled-up paper at the closest officer.

She tried to keep her tone light, as if she were amused by their shenanigans, but she didn't fool anyone, and the levity disappeared from the gathering. The brass was on the scene, so all the fun had come to a screeching halt. Uniforms who didn't belong started to drift away, one or two giving Taylor a sideways glance. She ignored them, the way she ignored most things these days.

As a patrol officer, she'd kept her head down, worked her cases, and developed a reputation for being a straight shooter. Her dedication and clean work had been rewarded with promotion after promotion; she was in plainclothes at twenty-eight. She'd caught a nasty first case in Homicide— the kidnapping and murder of a young girl. She'd nailed the bastard who'd done it; Richard Curtis was on death row now. The case made the national news and sent her career into overdrive. She quickly became known for being a hard-hitting investigator and moved up the ranks from detective to lead to sergeant, until she'd been given the plum job she had now—homicide lieutenant.

If her promotion to lieutenant at the tender age of thirty-four had rankled some of the more traditional officers on the force, the death of David Martin—one of their own—made it ten times worse. There were always going to be cops who tried to make her life difficult; it was part of being a chick on the force, part of having a reputation. Taylor was tough, smart, and liked to do things her own way to get the job done. The majority of the men she worked with had great respect for her abilities. There were always going to be detractors, cops who whispered behind her back, but in Taylor's mind, success trumped rumor every time.

Then Martin had decided to ruin her life and nearly derailed her career in the process. She was still clawing her way back.

Taylor's second in command, Detective Pete Fitzgerald,

lumbered toward her, the ever-present unlit cigarette hanging out of his mouth. He'd quit a couple of years before, after a minor heart attack, but kept one around to light in case of an emergency. Fitz had an impressive paunch; his belly reached Taylor before the rest of his body.

"Hey, LT. Sorry I had to drag you away from your beauty sleep." He looked her over, concern dawning in his eyes. "I was just kidding. What's up with you? You look like shit warmed over."

Taylor waved a hand in dismissal. "Didn't sleep. Aren't we supposed to have some sort of eclipse this morning? I think it's got me all out of whack."

Fitz took the hint and backed down. "Yeah, we are." He looked up quickly, shielding his eyes with his hand. "See, it's already started."

He was right. The moon was moving quickly across the sun, the crime scene darkening by the minute. "Eerie," she said.

He looked back at her, blinking hard. "No kidding. Remind me not to stare into the sun again."

"Will do. Celestial phenomenon aside, what do we have here?"

"Okay, darlin', here we go. We have a couple of lovebirds who decided to take an early morning stroll—found themselves a deceased Caucasian female on the Parthenon's steps. She's sitting up there pretty as you please, just leaning against the gate in front of the Parthenon doors like she sat down for a rest. Naked as a jaybird too, and very, very dead."

Taylor turned her gaze to the Parthenon. One of her favorite sites in Nashville, smack-dab in the middle of Centennial Park, the full-size replica was a huge draw for tourists and classicists alike. The statue of Athena inside was awe-inspiring. She couldn't count how many school field trips she'd been on here over the years. Leaving a body on the steps was one hell of a statement.

"Where are the witnesses?"

"Got the lovebirds separated, but the woman's having fits —we haven't been able to get a full statement. The scene's taped off. Traffic on West End has been blocked off, and we've closed all roads into and around Centennial Park. ME and her team have been here about fifteen minutes. Oh, and our killer was here at some point too." He grinned at her lopsidedly. "He dumped her sometime overnight, only the duckies and geese in the lake saw him. This is gonna be a bitch to canvass. Do you think we can admit 'AFLAC' as a statement in court?"

Taylor gave him a quick look and a perfunctory laugh, more amused at imagining Fitz waddling about like the duck from the insurance ads quacking than at his irreverent attitude. She knew better, but it did seem as if he was having a good time. Taylor understood that sometimes inappropriate attempts at humor were the only way a cop could make it through the day, so she chastised him gently. "You've got a sick sense of humor, Fitz." She sighed, turning off all personal thoughts, becoming a cop again. All business, all the time. That's what they needed to see from her.

"We'll probably have to go public and ask who was here last night and when, but I'm not holding my breath that we'll get anything helpful, so let's put it off for now."

He nodded in agreement. "Do you want to put up the chopper? Probably useless—whoever dumped her is long gone."

"I think you're right." She jerked her head toward the Parthenon steps. "What's he trying to tell us?"

Fitz looked toward the doors of the Parthenon, where the medical examiner was crouched over the naked body. His voice dropped, and he suddenly became serious. "I don't know, but this is going to get ugly, Taylor. I got a bad feeling."

Taylor held a hand up to cut him off. "C'mon, man, they're all ugly. It's too early to start spinning. Let's just get through the morning. Keep the frickin' media out of here—put 'em down in the duck shit if you have to. You can let them know which roads are closed so they can get the word out to their traffic helicopters, but that's it. Make sure the uniforms keep everyone off the tape. I don't want another soul in here until I have a chance to be fully briefed by all involved. Has the Park Police captain shown up yet?"

Fitz shook his head. "Nah. They've called him, but I haven't seen him."

"Well, find him, too. Make sure they know which end is up. Let's get the perimeter of this park searched, grid by grid, see if we find something. Get K-9 out here, let them do an article search. Since the roads are already shut off, tell them to expand the perimeter one thousand outside the borders of the park. I want to see them crawling around like ants at a picnic. I see any of them hanging in McDonald's before this is done, I'm kicking some butt."

Fitz gave her a mock salute. "I'm on it. When Sam determined she was dumped, I went ahead and called K-9, and pulled all the officers coming off duty. We may have an overtime situation, but I figured with your, um, finesse... " He snorted out the last word, and Taylor eyed him coolly.

"I'll handle it." She pushed her hair back from her face and reestablished her hurried ponytail. "Get them ready for all hell to break loose. I'm gonna go talk to Sam."

"Glad to serve, love. Now go see Sam, and let the rest of us grunts do our jobs. If you decide you want the whirlybird, give me a thumbs-up." He blew her a kiss and marched toward the command post, snapping his fingers at the officers to get their attention.

Turning toward the building, she caught a stare from one of the older patrols. His gaze was hostile, lip curled in a sneer. She gave him her most brilliant smile, making his scowl deepen. She broke off the look, shaking her head. She didn't have time to worry about politics right now.

CHAPTER 2

Taylor approached Sam cautiously, making sure she followed the ME's path to the body. They wouldn't be able to blame any loss of evidence on her. Pulling on her latex gloves, she tapped Sam lightly on the shoulder. Sam looked up. Anticipating Taylor's first question, she shook her head.

"There's no obvious cause of death—no stab wounds, no gunshot wounds. Evidence of rape. There's some bruising and tearing, a little bit of blood. He got her pretty good. There's some dirt on her, too. Wind probably blew some stuff around last night. I'll get a better idea when I get her open."

She rocked back on her heels and saw Taylor's face for the first time. "Girl, you look like crap. When's the last time you slept?"

"Been a while." The sleepless nights were catching up with her. She was almost thankful when a new case popped like this; the past slid away briefly when she could focus her attention elsewhere.

Sam gave her one last appraising glance. "Hmmph."

Dr. Samantha Owens had shoulder-length brown hair she always wore back in a ponytail, feminine wisps she couldn't control framing her face. She often joked that she'd rather look like a girl than a ghoul when she met someone new so the first impression wasn't one of horror. Taylor was always amused to see people scatter like rats when they found out the beautiful and composed woman was a professional pathologist. Most run-of-the-mill people didn't want to hang out with a woman who cut up dead bodies for a living.

Unlike many of the women she and Taylor had grown up with, Sam didn't join the Junior League, have beautiful babies, and lunch at Bread & Company. Instead, she spent her time perched over Nashville's endless supply of dead bodies, a position she was in much too often. She was also Taylor's best friend and was allowed liberties where others weren't.

"I've been telling you, you need to get some help."

"Hush up, Sam, I don't want to hear it. Tell me about our girl." Taylor let the knot in her stomach and the ache in her temples take complete hold. She had warmed up in the early-morning heat, but looking at the dead girl was giving her the chills. "Fitz said she was dumped?"

Sam traced an invisible line around the body with her finger. "Definitely. She wasn't killed here. See the livor pattern? The bottom of her legs, thighs and calves, her butt, the inside of her arms, and her back. The blood pooled in those areas. But she's sitting up, right? The lividity wouldn't present this way unless she had been chilling out on her back for a while. She was definitely dead for a few hours before she was dumped."

Taylor looked closely at the purplish-red blotches. In contrast, the front of the girl's body looked as pale and grimy as a dead jellyfish.

"No blood, either. Maybe he's a vampire." Sam leered briefly at Taylor, made fangs out of her fingers, hissed. Her morbid sense of humor always popped up at the most inappropriate times.

"You're insane."

"I know. No, he did her someplace else, then dumped her here." She looked around and said quietly, "Seriously, this feels very staged. She was put here for a reason, posed, everything. He wanted her found right away. The question is, why?"

Taylor didn't comment, but tucked Sam's remark into the back of her mind to be brought out and chewed on later. She knew it was worth thinking about; Sam had sound instincts. She turned back toward the command center. Seeing Fitz, she peeled the glove off her right hand, put two fingers in her mouth, and whistled sharply. He turned, and she shook her head. The helicopter definitely wasn't going to be needed.

Taylor looked back at the girl's face. So young. Another, so young. "Give me something to work with. Do you have a time of death?"

Sam thought for a moment. "Looking at her temp, she died sometime before midnight. Let's say ten to twelve hours ago, give or take. Rigor's still in, though she's starting to break up."

"Gives him time to kill her and get her here. Okay. Semen?"

"Oh yeah. It's all over the place. This guy really doesn't care about trying to be subtle. Not terribly bright. It shouldn't be too hard to match him up if he's in CODIS. He's certainly not holding anything back." She laughed at her pun, and Taylor couldn't help a brief smile.

"How about under her nails? Did she fight back?"

Sam lifted the dead girl's right hand. "I looked pretty closely, but I didn't see anything resembling skin or blood. I'll have them bag her hands and do scrapings back at the shop, but it doesn't look like she got hold of anything. We didn't find any ID with the body, so we'll print her and send them over to see if you can find a match. They'll be clear enough to run through AFIS."

Taylor was hardly listening. She stared at the girl's face. *So young*, she thought again. Man, there was going to be major fallout when they held this press conference. The statement started percolating in her head. *At six o'clock this morning, the body of a Caucasian female was discovered on the steps of the Parthenon...*

She looked back to Sam. "So no idea what killed her, huh?"

Sam relaxed, sitting back on her haunches. She stripped off her gloves and watched Taylor leaning in on the body.

"Hell if I know. Nothing's really jumping out at me. Give me a break, T, you know the drill."

"You'll get me all the pics yesterday, right? And do the post right now. I mean—"she attempted a more conciliatory tone, "—will you do the post right now?"

"I'll bump her to the top of the guest list. There's something else... Do you smell anything?"

"Just your perfume. Is it new?"

"See, that's the weird thing. I'm not wearing any. I think the smell is coming from the body. And I'll tell you, Taylor, this would be my first sweet-smelling corpse, you know?"

Taylor had noticed the scent. She inhaled sharply through her nose. Yes, there were all the usual stinks that came with a dead body: the unmistakable smell of decay, the stink of fear, the tang of stale urine and excrement. But overlaying all these olfactory wonders was a tangy sweetness. She thought hard for a moment, searching for the memory the smell triggered. The scent was somehow familiar, almost like —That was it!

"Sam, you know what this smells like? The spa across the way, Essential Therapy. Remember, I gave you a gift certificate for a massage there for your birthday? They have all those lotions and soaps and essential oil candles... "

"Wait a minute. You're right. She smells like incense." She stared at the body. "What if... Okay, give me a second here." Sam reached into her kit and extracted a small pair of tweezers. She bent over and started picking through the dirt on the body.

"What are you doing?" Taylor watched Sam put a few pieces of leaves and sticks into a small white paper bag. Somewhat disgusted, she watched Sam shove her nose into the bag and breathe in deeply. "Ugh, Sam."

"No, here." Sam's eyes lit up, and Taylor was tempted to back away. But Sam grabbed her hand and shoved the bag toward her face. "Really, smell."

Taylor wrinkled her nose, swallowing hard. It was one thing seeing the body and smelling it from a few feet away, but sticking her nose into the detritus that came from the body itself was totally gross. Grimacing, she took the bag and inhaled. The scent was smoky and floral, not at all unpleasant.

Sam's eyes were shining in excitement. "This isn't dirt, Taylor. These are herbs. She has herbs scattered all over her body. Now what the hell is that all about?"

Taylor shook her head slowly, trying to absorb the new discovery. "I don't know. Can you isolate which herb it is?"

"Yeah, I can let a buddy of mine at UT in Knoxville take a look. He's head of the university's botany department and totally into all this stuff. I don't think it's just one herb, though. The leaves are all different sizes and shapes. Oh man, this is too cool."

"Sam, you're awful." Taylor couldn't stop herself from smiling. "You like this job too much."

"That's why I'm good at it. Tim's our lead 'gator today. I'm going to get him set up here to bag all this stuff, and I'll have a runner take it up to UT ASAP. You know, it would be a lot simpler if that idiot mayor would help us get our own lab capable of handling this kind of stuff. Hell, it'd be nice if we could even do tox screens in-house."

Sam continued grumbling under her breath and stood up, signaling the end of the conversation. She waved to her team, calling them over. The body was ready to be moved.

"Wait, Sam. Did Crime Scene pick up anything else? Clothes, jewelry?"

"Not yet, but you're in their way. She's got enough of this crap on her that it's gonna take them a while to collect it all. Why don't you go back and try to find out who this girl is for me, okay? Y'all need to catch this guy, 'cause once the press gets a hold of this, they're gonna freak the whole city. It's not every day I have to come to the middle of Centennial Park to collect a body, much less for a staged crime scene. Look at the vultures hovering already."

She swept her hand toward the media trucks. Their level of activity had picked up, excitement palpable in the air. Techs were setting up lights and running around on the street by the duck pond, with cameras and portable microphones in tow. The news vans were lined up around the corner. Taylor watched Fitz and the patrol officers struggle to keep the reporters from rushing the tape to gather their precious scoops. Nothing like murder in the morning to start a feeding frenzy.

"Seriously, Taylor, you know how they are. They'll find some way to spin this into a grand conspiracy and warn all the parents to keep their girls at home until you catch whoever did this." She started grumbling. "It should be frickin' illegal for the chief to have given them their own radios. Now every newsie in Nashville hovers over my shoulder while I scope a body."

Taylor lowered her eyelids for a second and gave her best

friend a half smile. "Well, honey, if it makes you feel any better, all the talking heads and their cameramen are squishing through goose poo trying to get their stories. Guess Lake Watauga has its purposes after all. Call me as soon as you have anything."

Sam laughed. "Yeah, yeah. Split. You're making me nervous."

Like what you've read so far?
Click here to keep reading FIELD OF GRAVES!

THE ABANDONED HEART
BY LAURA BENEDICT

EXCLUSIVE EXCERPT

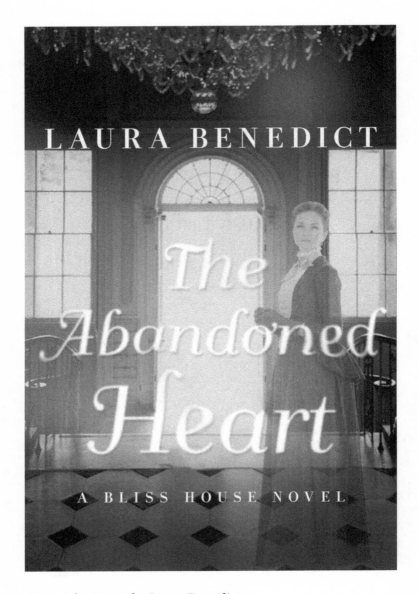

LAURA BENEDICT

The Abandoned Heart

A BLISS HOUSE NOVEL

"Murder, sexual obsession, and misogyny explode in the final scenes, bringing all the simmering evil to the surface in a shocking finale, that, like all good horror stories, is probably not the end. You just can't look away from this bomb site—nor forget it. Dripping with southern gothic atmosphere."

–*Booklist,* starred review, on CHARLOTTE'S STORY

"Set in 1957 in southern Virginia, Benedict's suspenseful, atmospheric follow-up to 2014's *Bliss House* finds housewife Charlotte Bliss devastated by the death of her four-year-old daughter... A satisfyingly creepy tale for a rainy night."

–*Publisher's Weekly* on CHARLOTTE'S STORY

"An evocative, frightening and flawless gothic, CHARLOTTE'S STORY is guaranteed to send a delicious chill down your spine. Nobody does more for the modern southern gothic than Laura Benedict."

–J.T. Ellison, *New York Times* bestselling author of WHAT LIES BEHIND

"Benedict writes with passion and authority. CHARLOTTE'S STORY is not to be missed."

–Carolyn Haines, author of the *Sarah Booth Delaney Bones Mysteries*, including BONE TO BE WILD

ABOUT LAURA

Laura Benedict is the author of the Bliss House series of dark suspense novels, CHARLOTTE'S STORY, BLISS HOUSE, and THE ABANDONED HEART (Pegasus Crime), as well as DEVIL'S OVEN, a modern Frankenstein tale, ISABELLA MOON, and CALLING MR. LONELY HEARTS (Ballantine). Her work has appeared in Ellery Queen Mystery Magazine, PANK, and numerous anthologies like THRILLERS: 100 MUST-READS (Oceanview), and SLICES OF FLESH (Dark Moon Books). She originated and edited the Surreal South Anthology of Short Fiction Series with her husband, Pinckney Benedict, and edited FEEDING KATE, a charity anthology, for their press, Gallowstree Press. A Cincinnati, Ohio native, Laura grew up in Louisville, Kentucky, and claims both as hometowns. She currently lives with her family in the southern wilds of a Midwestern state, surrounded by bobcats, coyotes, and other less picturesque predators. Find out more, enter her monthly contests, and follow her blog at laurabenedict.com.

PROLOGUE

It was the spring of 1876, and the first families of Old Gate, Virginia, were putting on quite a show for the man from New York who meant to be their new neighbor. The world was not such a large place that someone from a good Virginia family did not have connections in New York who could make *inquiries* about such a man. So everyone in the county already knew that Randolph Hasbrouck Bliss was about thirty years old, the son of a man who was reputed to have made an enormous fortune buying cotton from farmers in the Confederate States (sometimes from the government itself) for resale to the Northern textile mills, and then selling arms and ammunition back to the Confederacy. That he had a wife who was, interestingly, several years older than he, and a young daughter who, it was said, wasn't quite right in the head. That he had been educated at the College of New Jersey, and, after having shown some skill in managing one of his father's import operations (French wines, and more textiles), had decided to try his hand at farming apples and peaches in central Virginia. Those who had made the *inquiries* hadn't been able to find out exactly why he had decided to change careers, but there were whispers that he had *habits* of a nature that embarrassed and displeased his mother, who was from old Dutch New York stock. It was believed that those *habits* involved women. Often much younger women, and women of ill repute.

But the dinner guests at Maplewood, the gracious, pillar-fronted home of Katharine "Pinky" Archer and her husband, Robert, found their prejudices undermined as soon as they met Randolph.

He wasn't a man whom any woman would particularly call handsome, with features that were heavy and decidedly non-patrician: a prominent nose and thick, dark brows. But his jaw was strong and his brown eyes alert and lively. He wore his clothes well, despite having a waist that did not taper much from his broad shoulders, and an overall frame that was more like that of a laborer than of a man who spent his days giving orders to others. Like every other man in the room, he was dressed in a double-breasted evening coat of black, with matching trousers. His silk waistcoat was a rich shade of peacock blue that was at once daring and elegant. They could see that everything he wore was of superior quality, and though his face was rather common, he inhabited his expensive clothes with an easy, animal grace.

After a dinner that included expected delights of smoked oysters, turtle soup, bison, and a French cream tart, the Reverend Edward M. Searle and a couple of the other men of Old Gate watched Randolph with interest as he stood, smiling, surrounded by women. The women, including Edward's wife, Selina, and their hostess, Pinky Archer, preened under Randolph's gaze. His compliments were easy and witty. Was it that gaze that attracted them? As he looked at each woman, he seemed to give her his undivided attention, and when he looked elsewhere, she would wilt a bit. The women's attraction to Randolph was puzzling to all of the men, and, if they had spoken to one another about it, they might have agreed that it had something to do with the juxtaposition of his wealth and his common appearance. Or was it the uneasy sense that he was capable of doing the unpredictable?

When Pinky sat down at the piano, she asked who would be willing to sing "Silver Threads Among the Gold," as she had recently learned it, and Randolph volunteered readily. He sang confidently in a bold, baritone voice, but showed a strong degree of modesty when the group—particularly the women—applauded enthusiastically at the song's end. One of the older women, Pinky's mother, dabbed discreetly at her eye with a handkerchief.

When the singing was done, the party broke into smaller groups. Some played cards, others gathered around the enormous book of drawings of New York scenery that Randolph had sent as a gift to his hostess. With most of the women occupied, Edward, who was the priest at St. Anselm's Episcopal Church, saw his opportunity to speak to Randolph alone.

A servant had brought Randolph a glass of water, and he was finishing it when Edward approached. He spoke quietly. "Randolph, won't you walk outside with me for a moment? The evening is fine, and I like to take a small stroll after a large meal. Maplewood's garden is quite fragrant in the evening."

Randolph smiled, his dark eyes full of mischief. "Are you sure you wouldn't rather take a turn with one of these beautiful ladies, Edward? Your wife looks very becoming. In fact all the women I've met since I arrived in Old Gate are possessed of charms unseen where I come from in New York. And I warn you. I won't sit still if you try to kiss me beneath a rose bower."

Robert Archer, their host, was passing and chanced to hear Randolph's response. He stopped, chuckling. "You can trust Edward. I've known him since we were boys, and he never tried to kiss me once."

A slight look of irritation passed over Edward's face, but he banished it quickly and, with feigned gruffness, said, "But you haven't Randolph's exotic Yankee charm, Robert. Familiarity breeds contempt, as I'm sure you'll agree."

"Scoundrel. Don't be long with your stroll, gentlemen. I fear the ladies will not tolerate Randolph being away from them much longer." He laid his hand on Randolph's broad back in a gesture of camaraderie that was not quite a slap. "You've become quite the favorite already. You'll have to tell me your secret sometime. My Pinky and I have only been married five years, yet sometimes I think that since I've passed the age of thirty she sees me as ready for the ash heap. Beware, Randolph. The young women of the county are a flirtatious set, but we love them dearly, don't we, Edward?"

Edward nodded sagely and guided Randolph to the door.

Outside, the evening was indeed fine, and the cloudless sky above Maplewood was a brocade of countless stars.

"You can't see the sky like this in New York, in the city." Randolph stopped on the garden's path and looked up. "Too many factories, too many lights. My wife, Amelia, will like it here very much. She is reluctant to leave Long Island, but I think she and my daughter will be happy in the end. I have a working design for Bliss House, though it is sure to take more than a year to build."

Edward cleared his throat. "Some would say Old Gate is a bit rough around the edges, but I was happy to come back here after the war and seminary."

"I can't think of a better place to build new traditions for myself and my family. Sometimes a man needs to escape the bonds of family tradition, don't you agree?"

"Then I would say you will find its isolation to your liking.

Old Gate is not like other Virginia towns. We are an insular place. The people who settled here, rather than in larger places like Lynchburg or Charlottesville, came here—or come here—because they were either not wanted in those larger societies or had reasons of their own for absenting themselves." He looked closely at Randolph. "What are your reasons for wanting to come to a place as remote as Old Gate?"

Randolph smiled and gave a small laugh. "I suppose I want a change. Nothing wrong with that, is there? As I said, sometimes the bonds of family can become too tight."

Rather than pressing him further, Edward glanced over his shoulder to see if they were being followed and continued walking. "This way, please." When he was satisfied that they were far enough away from the house, he stopped again. He was several inches taller than Randolph, and the moonlight sharpened his patrician profile: a high, Grecian nose, tall forehead, and chiseled chin. His prominent height intimidated many people.

Randolph looked up at him without any sign of anxiety. "Is something troubling you? I'll be of assistance if I can."

"My friends would not thank me for speaking with you. While I am of their society, they hold somewhat more jaundiced views than I on many things." He shook his head. "I would never accuse them of a lack of integrity, but I fear that the trio of individuals who own the property you are about to purchase for your home has not been completely honest with you."

Randolph laughed. "It is business. No business can be conducted in complete honesty. Nothing would ever be settled. Do you think the price they ask is too dear? It seems quite reasonable to me. It's a prime bit of land. Perfect for orchards, and an excellent home site."

"If it is so excellent, is it credible to you that it should be so close to town and as yet undeveloped? We have undergone much improvement since the war."

"Is there some defect I should know of? I have found none. Monsieur Hulot, my architect, has approved the surveyor's report, and will depart with his assistant from France at my telegram. I have spent much time at the site. I am satisfied. What is this, Edward?" Randolph assumed a joshing tone. "Is there some other bidder you want it for? I'm not afraid of paying a bit more to ensure that I have it. Or—" He seemed to consider for a moment. "Is it that my erstwhile neighbors are disturbed because they've learned that the distinguished Monsieur Hulot happens to be a Negro?"

Edward gave a little cough. "I'm sure that has never come up."

"Then just tell me what it is you have to tell me."

"Very well," Edward said. "A lot of the old families struggle to keep up their homes. The ones farming tobacco are just recovering. They need the money. Your money."

"Seems a fair trade."

"That particular farm was never planted with tobacco. It was part of an early land grant, and the owners leased different parts of it to many tenants over the years. When I was a boy, it was home to the Doyle family, a family with Quaker sympathies."

"Quakers? Here?"

"The Doyles were friendly with the Quaker group down in Lynchburg. And as you probably know, the Quakers had no sympathy for slaveholding and subverted it in every way they could. Old Gate was on the route from Lynchburg to Culpeper County, which was a kind of gathering point for runaway slaves headed north."

"Is there anywhere here that isn't touched by that kind of history? We must move past the war, man. It's our duty."

"Please, listen. We need to go back inside soon." Now

Edward was brusque. "There was a house and a barn on the property, and the house had a shed attached to it. Sometime in 1847 or '48, the Doyles began to hide runaway slaves who were on their way north, in that shed. It became a kind of open secret among certain people in Old Gate."

Randolph nodded. "That sounds like it was virtuous, but dangerous."

"There are people in this house tonight whose parents didn't like what the Doyles and the Quakers were doing. People who didn't want to lose their own slaves because of such subversion close to home. Randolph, a group of Old Gate men surrounded the property one night and set fire to both the house and shed. When the family and, it's said, two female slaves and their children tried to escape, the men held them at gunpoint until they went back inside the buildings. If they didn't, they shot them dead, right there."

In their own momentary silence, they heard a woman's laughter from the house.

"It's a terrible story, but it has nothing to do with me. I thank you for telling me, Edward. Was anyone prosecuted?"

"Of course not. It was done at night, and there were no witnesses left. No one is really even sure how many were killed. Eight, maybe ten people."

"I see."

"No, I don't think you do. A few years later, another house was built there, on that same site. But no one was able to live in it for more than a few months at a time. Everyone who lived in that house suffered some tragedy, and they were forced to leave. Suicides. Madness. A murder."

Randolph scoffed. "That's bald superstition, and quite ridiculous. You're an educated man. Surely you don't believe in such things. Superstition is the stuff of old women and parlor games. To be honest, I'm amused by the superstitious aspects of the old pagan rites. Why, the Romans were a noble bunch, and the Celtics, too. But ghosts? That's nonsense."

Edward stiffened. "You would put your family at risk?"

"Of course not. There *is* no risk. There's nothing left of any buildings there except traces of a foundation. And that will be dug up before any building begins. I dare any curse to try to cling to me. It would find that I am not so easily cowed."

"I wish you would listen. There are other farms to be had."

"We should go back inside, Edward. It's growing late." Edward's shoulders fell, and he shook his head. They started back to the house. Not wanting to leave his new friend dispirited, Randolph made an effort to acknowledge his obviously genuine concern. "As a priest, perhaps you could perform some sort of blessing on the land. Might that not help obviate any curse, or whatever seems to be going on?"

Edward stopped. "I dislike that the Old Gate parties involved in this sale have not been frank with you. They seem to take it as rather a joke that someone like you—someone from a part of the country that they revile—is paying good money for the site of such an atrocity. You do not have true friends here, I'm afraid, Randolph. I don't know that they will ever be different if you choose to build your house here."

The light from the salon touched Randolph, illuminating his not quite handsome face. When Edward looked down into those eyes, he wasn't sure if the sincerity he saw there was true or skillful manipulation. There was something else, too, something harder, that he hadn't seen when they were in the house.

"I hope I may consider *you* my friend." Randolph rested his hand on the taller man's back, just as Robert Archer had touched *him* in friendship, and Edward felt an unpleasant sensation of cold spread over his body.

An hour later, the party broke up with many promises for future invitations. Randolph was heartily enjoined to write to his new friends just as soon as he knew when he would be returning to Old Gate to begin building his new home.

As he settled into the coach that would take him back to Missus Green's Inn and Boardinghouse near the center of town, Randolph felt in the left pocket of his waistcoat for his matches. The matches were there, but there was something else: a small, folded note, which, when opened and held close to the flame of a lighted match, was revealed to be an invitation of a particularly intimate sort, written in a delicate, well-formed hand. He smiled. It was an invitation he would gladly accept.

He blew out the match and settled back in the seat. Yes. He was very much looking forward to settling in Old Gate.

CHAPTER 1

Lucy
Walpurgisnacht, 1924

Lucy Bliss ran blindly through the moonlit rose garden, thorns grabbing at her as though they would keep her from leaving. As she reached the break in the garden wall that would lead her to the woods, her robe tangled on the last bush, so she tore it from her body with a cry and left it behind. Was someone following? Surely Randolph, who was as frail as a man risen from a grave of five years, could not capture her.

My husband risen from his grave! So much is explained. The voices in the night. The light near the springhouse. How did I not see?

Above the trees the distant lights of Old Gate shone silver on the scattered clouds. Only twenty-five years earlier, before she had married Randolph in 1899, there had been but a dozen gas streetlamps in town, and the night sky had looked endless and cluttered with stars. How different it had been. Walking with her friends to the little theater, or home from a party, her laughing voice louder than she knew was proper. But she hadn't cared. She had been cheerfully rebellious, happy to disregard her mother's constant instructions about minding her behavior, and her father's lectures from both his Episcopal pulpit and the dinner table. Though they were rigid people, and difficult to love, she had loved them both, and had obeyed—to a point. Few things were ever serious to her in those days. It had all been in fun.

Bright. Her life had been so wonderfully bright.

Now she was well into her forties, and her life had dimmed. Her feet were bare, tender from running over the crushed shells on the winding garden paths beside Bliss House, and her breath came in bursts. From moment to moment she wasn't sure if she were dreaming or not. Before she'd gone to bed, Terrance, who had run Bliss House for her these past few years, and was no older than she, had given her the medicine that helped her feel calm, helped her forget. But she had terrible dreams and often woke to find that she had chewed the knuckle of her finger until it bled and there were tears on her cheeks. Now, dreaming or awake, she had fled the house, running, running. For months she had been loath to walk outside. Loath to leave her room. How she had run when she was a child! And when her son, Michael Searle, was young, they had run through the orchards together, playing and racing, far from Randolph's critical gaze.

Michael Searle, my son. But more than a son. A gift.

This very night he was on his way home from North Carolina, where he had been visiting the woman he would marry. She had to get somewhere safe, to warn him—before he arrived—never to return to Bliss House.

Your father is alive! He will steal your happiness, my sweet child.

The path into the woods was crowded with brush and

newly red switches of wild blackberry, whose thorns were even more ambitious and brutal than those of the roses. She slowed. Her thin, torn gown was no protection from the cool night, and a layer of sweat caused her to shiver violently. Craving the former safety of her own bed within her flower-covered bedroom walls, she thought of sinking to the ground, nesting in the brambles like an animal. Still, she pushed deeper into the woods, even though no one seemed to be coming after her.

Do they think I am weak, that I will come crawling back?

As a girl, she had thought of Bliss House as a mysterious, magical place, all the more fascinating because her parents had told her to stay away. Now she knew every inch of its shining wood floors and paneled walls. She had danced in the ballroom dozens of times, and hurried up and down the staircases twenty times a day, and aired the rooms, and watered flowers and written letters at her desk in the morning room, and rocked her son to sleep, and wiped his brow, and entertained friends, and listened to the bees drowsing over the roses, and watched her husband, the man who had built Bliss House, go slowly mad. And she had lived in the presence of ghosts, and had even ceased to be afraid of them.

But if Randolph were alive—truly alive—she would have to live in fear.

Again. It didn't matter if she were awake or dreaming. She would rather die than live with Randolph. Again.

Ahead, in the trees, there was a quivering light where there should not have been a light. Lucy glanced again over her shoulder to make sure she hadn't gotten turned around, but there was Bliss House rising tall and threatening behind her, its windows glowing warmly as though it were still a safe place. A place where, sometimes, she was happy.

Thank God Michael Searle is away. I will keep him safe.

Yes. Ahead of her was a light where there was supposed to be nothing, and desperation carried her toward it.

Are you hooked yet?

Devour the rest of THE ABANDONED HEART, available wherever books are sold!

Printed in the USA
CPSIA information can be obtained
at www.ICGtesting.com
LVHW05173825O324
775469LV00007B/264